Highland Wolf Pact: Blood Reign

By Selena Kitt

eXcessica publishing

Highland Wolf Pact: Blood Reign © 2015 by Selena Kitt

Excessica LLC
486 S Ripley #164
Alpena MI 49707

To order additional copies of this book, contact:
books@excessicapublishing.com
www.excessica.com

Cover art © 2015 Taria Reed
First Edition 2015

Chapter One

Griff could smell them, not far behind.

Gaining.

He couldn't let that happen.

He signaled his men, using a low grunt and a soft growl. Rory MacFalon heard him and followed his hand signal, breaking right through the trees. The forest cover was thick and the horses didn't always find their footing, but the path they'd tracked through the woods—their own shortcut—was perfect for this purpose. Griff grinned—to an outsider, it would have looked like a snarl, his snout long, teeth drawn back—as he watched Rory slow in the underbrush, awaiting his next command.

They were going to make it. He could feel it, something instinctual.

He barked an order to Garaith, who gave a nod with his big, shaggy black head, giving Griff a grin that also looked much like a snarl, and he, too, broke off and joined Rory on the side of the path. The rest of his pack of wulver warriors—half-men, half-wolves, wearing full Scots armor and riding horses through the MacFalon forest—followed Griff's lead as he pulled his giant war horse aside, waving them past. They knew the shortcut as well as he did—they'd helped him create it.

"Cam!" Griff called to one of his teammates, who brought up the rear of the pack. Cam slowed his horse, surprised when Griff tossed him the giant rack of buck antlers he was carrying. "Take them to the safe area. Lead the team! Go!"

Horse hooves thundered through the forest. If the other two packs didn't know where the shortcut was, they would now. But it didn't matter, because Griff knew they were going to win.

He barked orders to Rory and Garaith to follow him. They needed more space than they had in the woods to end this thing properly. The two wulvers fell in behind him. Griff dug the heels of his boots into Uri's side, leaning over his powerful neck as the horse tore up the path and broke through the trees. His team, he noted with satisfaction, was already corralled in the "safe" area. There were wulver women gathered at the mouth of their den, watching with bright eyes as the warriors burst into the field.

Griff gave a war whoop, turning his mount to face the other two oncoming teams. He directed Rory and Garaith toward the first—both had already drawn their swords. They were wooden, just training swords, a fact that bothered Griff a great deal, but his father had insisted. His mother had protested as well—and he could understand a woman's protest, that someone might get hurt—but his father, Raife, was the pack's leader, and some day, Griff would take his place. Wasn't it about time they were allowed to use real swords? Even if it was just for this, the Great Hunt. It only happened once a year, after all.

Two dozen wulver warriors charged into the clearing, and Griff heard the women squeal and yelp as swords began to clash. Rory and Garaith were his best fighters by far, and they could hold their own against any of the rest. He saw them fighting off a dozen menacing pack members, while Griff himself took on the other dozen or so that had begun to circle.

Not that he let that stop him.

Griff swung his sword expertly. They all had wooden swords, so it was a fair fight. Not that twelve against one was fair, exactly, but it was what he'd planned. The antlers—their prize—and the rest of his men were safe. He had his two best fighters—who had already bested half the other pack—and he didn't doubt his own ability for a moment.

Even when he was surrounded. And he was. He'd bested three of them already, but there were more, and they circled him. Griff's horse pawed the ground, nervous, but he kept Uri under control, swinging his sword at all comers. And they came. Wulver after wulver, snarling and swinging, snapping their jaws and howling. Griff didn't hesitate. Three more wulvers had to fall back because his sword had slipped through and, wooden or not, dented their breast-plates—a "kill" shot.

He could hear the other wulvers, spectators, howling their approval. The women especially. They were all excited to watch the men compete. He knew his mother was among them, watching—with breath held, wringing her hands, no doubt. Sibyl might be married to the pack leader, but she'd never gotten used to or really understood the wulver warrior's constant training. She was human, and a woman. He could forgive her that.

Not that he was winning for her—or any of the wulver women he saw jumping up and down and clapping as he bested another of the rival team. Griff won because it was part of him. Winning was everything. To him, losing didn't mean just losing. Losing meant death. He didn't care if it was a wooden sword to his breast plate or an actual arrow whizzing by his head. It was all death.

He didn't even realize it was over until he saw Rory and Garaith, who had taken down the last of the other team, dismounting and charging across the field toward him. Griff howled in triumph, sliding off his horse and clapping his teammates on the back. He shook his head, much like a dog who shakes off when it comes out of a lake, and heard all the girls sigh and exclaim as his features transformed from wolf to human once again. Many of the wulver women looked at him hungrily, giving him those appreciative, over-the-shoulder glances that meant they were open to... well, anything. He'd likely take one, or maybe two or three, of them up on that later. But for now, he was too interested in basking in the glory.

"We did it!" Garaith yelled, giving Griff a one-armed squeeze.

From the "safe" zone, Griff's teammates roared their approval. Rory threw back his dark head and howled, too, although Griff saw he was quick to change from wulver-warrior back to human as his mother rushed across the field to hug him. Kirstin was followed by her husband, Donal—The MacFalon. It was their land the wulvers' den resided on. They both congratulated their wulver-warrior son on a job well done, and Rory stood there grinning like a fool. Griff wondered if the grin plastered to his own face looked just as ridiculous.

Even Griff's bested pack-mates congratulated him, albeit a little grudgingly, on a good win. Griff saw his mother, her red hair starting to be streaked at the temples with a few gray strands, standing near the entrance of their den, watching. She was smiling, but it was a strained smile. She hated the fighting, he knew. He gave her a wink, grinning, and her smile brightened just a little.

Beside her, Garaith's mother, Laina, her white-blonde hair braided behind her like his mother's, waved to her son. There was no hesitation in Laina about her son's warrior ways. She was wulver through and through, and appreciated her son's prowess on the battlefield—training exercise or not. That made him think of his uncle, Darrow—Garaith's father—who had been overseeing the Great Hunt, along with Darrow's brother, Raife. Darrow was Raife's second in command. The last he'd seen them, Griff had been leading his pack, holding the antlers high, and riding hard to get back to the safe zone.

Then Griff couldn't see anyone because he was being surrounded again, this time by well-wishers who clapped him on the back and wulver women who kissed his cheek and rubbed up against him as close as they could get. Griff enjoyed the attention although he didn't exactly bask in it. Winning had been a foregone conclusion as far as he was concerned.

"What in the gory hell did you think you were doing?" Raife's voice thundered through the clearing as he galloped up on his charger. Their pack leader could command anything, whether it was one man, a room full of people, or an entire army. Just the sound of his voice booming over the field got everyone's attention. Griff sighed inwardly, if not outwardly, glancing up to see his father's horse pulling up short of the crowd. Darrow was close behind. "Is that what you think leading looks like? You fall back to hold off the enemy, and sacrifice yourself?"

"I won, didn't I?" Griff shot back, feeling his cheeks go hot as he met his father's dark gaze. He heard some murmurs in the crowd, and knew what they were looking at. Any time Griff got angry, they told him his eyes would flash red. Literally. It had been that way since he was a baby, his mother said. There was something in the wulver lore about a prophecy, and a "red wulver,"—which he was, when he changed to wolf—a big, red wolf. He couldn't hide his coloring, but the red eyes he'd learned to control over the years. Somehow, though, his father always managed to bring out the worst in him.

"I beat them all!"

"Winning isn't everything!" Raife snapped. "A pack leader has more to think about than just winning! A stunt like that can cost a pack their leader. And a leaderless pack is a dead pack!"

Griff blinked at his father, feeling heat spreading to his chest. So mayhaps it had been a little reckless. Mayhaps his plan, while successful, had endangered not only him, but Rory and Garaith as well. He felt a little guilty about that. But they'd done all right, even by themselves, hadn't they?

"It's just a game," Griff grumbled, and knew he was attempting to deflect his own public shaming when he tossed his chipped, splintering wooden sword to the grass. "These aren't even real weapons!"

"It's never just a game!" Raife roared. "A pack leader—ANY wulver warrior—can never afford to think of training as a game. The pack we live in is the last of our kind. We are the last of the wulvers. Most humans would kill the last of us out of fear alone."

I should jus' take ye on right now, ol' man. Raife wasn't really old, not in human or wulver years. He could lead their pack for another thirty or forty, if he wanted to. More's the pity, because Griff felt ready to lead now. He felt it in every fiber of his being, all the way to his bones.

Griff glared at his father, seeing his jaw harden. Had he guessed what Griff was thinking?

"You want this?" Raife's voice lowered as he leaned into his horse, toward his son. So he had guessed. The heat filling Griff's face intensified and he tried to control it. His father's eyes weren't red, they were wulver blue—all wulvers had blue eyes—but they got dark as a bottomless ocean when he was angry. And he was angry now. "Come get it. By law, you can challenge me any time to take the lead."

Griff felt the urge to challenge him tingling in his limbs, pricking him like a thousand little needles all over his body. The hair on the back of his neck stood up and he felt a growl building in his throat. He wouldn't be able to control it in a minute and he wondered who would win if he challenged his father now. There were no guarantees, but he thought he just might win.

Then he glanced over at his uncle, sitting on a horse beside Raife, and he wondered why Darrow had never challenged for the pack leader position. Was he so afraid to lose? Or—mayhaps, he was afraid he'd win? Darrow met his eyes and he saw a warning there. Don't do it, not now, not yet. But Griff felt ready. His body sang with his desire to lead, to conquer, to win.

"Son, I'd love to turn my role over to you," Raife told him, dismounting and looking around at the crowd of wulvers that watched, tense, waiting. "Some day, I hope I will. But right now, I know my leadership is still what's best for this pack. And I would do anything to protect it. Would you?"

Griff did growl at that. How could his father believe he wouldn't do everything to protect the pack? It was what he was born, bred and trained for. The Great Hunt was practice for war—a war that just might come, one day. He would be ready to take anyone on, to protect all of them—his mother, his sisters, his aunts, uncles, and cousins. Just like he was ready, right now, to take on his father.

They faced each other, man to man, the same height, same build. No one would have questioned that they weren't father and son, with the same big, brawny shoulders, strong jaws, thick, long, dark hair—Griff had been born a redhead, like his mother, but his newborn hair had changed color. He was still the only red wolf in the pack, though. And his eyes, instead of the blue of his father's, were actually a strange amber color that went red when he was emotional or angry, if others were to be believed. He'd never seen his own eyes turn color himself.

Both men were in full gear, although Raife had an actual sword at his side, while Griff's wooden one lay between them on the grass. He felt both excitement and worry rising in the crowd. Would there be a challenge this day? Would father and son face off in a duel that could lead to the death of one of the two big men? Griff heard a soft cry from near the mouth of the den, and knew his mother's voice well. She didn't want this to happen—likely, ever. But a man had to become a man eventually, didn't he?

"Winners get served first at the feast!" Laina, Griff's still very beautiful, shapely blonde aunt announced, putting an arm around Garaith, her son. "But don't they have to muck out the stalls first?"

Garaith grumbled and rolled his eyes at that and Griff caught his best friend's glance. Garaith was Darrow's son, a few years older than Griff, but like his father, he had a tendency to go off half-cocked. Griff might do things that were risky—but he never made a decision without thinking it through thoroughly first. Even in that moment, when he felt his anger building and his desire to challenge their pack leader to a fight, he weighed all his options before reacting.

"Garaith and Rory, you were outstanding following your leader's direction." Raife praised both of the young men, clapping them each on the back with a smile. "Even if your leader made a risky move."

Griff let it slide, swallowing his anger, but Raife's words hit home. He would die for Garaith or Rory or any of his team or pack mates. But when his father gave him that knowing look, he understood, finally, what the old man had been so angry about. Griff's strategy had won them the competition, certainly. But it had also been very risky. Had they been using real swords, instead of wooden ones, he wondered if the outcome might have been different. And that's the doubt he saw when he looked into his father's eyes.

"Aye, take the horses to the barn and muck out the stalls," Raife ordered. "Remember, serving the pack is what will keep you humble. And you always have to keep the pack foremost in your mind."

He looked at Griff as he said this last, and Griff gave him a nod, grabbing the reins of both his own horse and Raife's big stallion. His father's hand slipped onto his shoulder, squeezing briefly, and Raife spoke the words, just for him, "I'm proud of you, Griff. You're a good wulver and a fine man."

"Hurry back!" Sibyl called over the crowd at Griff, his shoulders drooping less than they'd been just a few minutes before. "Dinner's waiting!"

"Congratulations to the winners!" Donal MacFalon called, smiling as he watched his son, Rory, taking the reins of the horses. "I'm proud of all of you. Clan MacFalon has a surprise for all the winners when ye return, so do'na tarry long, boys!"

"Boys." Rory sighed, glancing over his shoulder at his father. "When are they going to start seeing us as men?"

"At least he didn't call you out in front of the whole pack," Griff grumbled as their team mates started gathering up the rest of the horses. "And ye're lucky—ye know ye'll be the laird of Clan MacFalon someday. Ye've got no one to challenge ye."

Griff gave Garaith a knowing look. As brothers, Darrow and Raife had worked side by side for years, Raife as alpha, Darrow his second. Griff didn't have any brothers, but he knew it was likely that someday, he would lead the pack, and Garaith would follow him, just like Darrow followed Raife.

"Ha, m'sister, Eilis, would have somethin' to say 'bout that." Rory laughed. He was so much like his father, good-humored, always smiling—even when he was facing his enemies. But he was deadly with a sword, and eerily accurate with his bow.

"Yer da would really let a woman lead yer clan?" Garaith asked, even though he knew as well as Griff did that the Scots had no qualms about letting a woman step into that role.

"Aye," Rory agreed with a nod. "But m'da wants t'marry Eilis off t'some English fop, last I heard, so she'll likely be givin' him heirs a'fore the year's through."

"Aye? Is that so?" Garaith bristled at this news.

Griff knew that Garaith had his eye on Eilis—since they were just pups, even though Rory's sister wasn't a wulver. It wasn't unheard of for wulvers and humans to mate. Griff's own mother was a human woman, as was Rory's father. His mother, Kirstin, had once been a wulver, but had taken a "cure" that Sibyl had developed for the wulver woman's curse of changing once a month due to estrus, or when she gave birth. The "cure" had worked all too well—Kirstin was now unable to change to wulver form at all.

Rory, Kirstin's first child with The MacFalon, had been quite a surprise to everyone, except maybe the midwife Beitrus, who had delivered Rory, when he came out as a wulver pup and not a human baby. Beitrus said Rory must have been conceived just at the cusp of Kirstin's change—completely out of her control—from human woman to wolf form.

"If ye want 'er, ye better tell m'father, or he's goin' t'send 'er to England and let King Henry pick t'richest match fer her," Rory warned his friend as they trudged up the hill.

"Aye," Garaith agreed, his eyes flashing. "I'll talk t'him."

Griff shook his head.

He liked women well enough, but he'd never mooned over them the way Garaith did over Eilis, or for that matter, the way Rory did over Griff's little sister, Maire. Griff could always have his pick of the litter—and he had picked, frankly, more than once—but he'd never found a girl who could keep his attention for longer than it took him to catch them. There were some in the pack who still believed in the idea of "one true mate," but Griff didn't hold to such silliness.

"C'mon, let's go," he told his two best friends as they mounted their own horses and started rounding up the rest. "I'm starvin' and I can'na wait t'get served first tonight. We earned it."

Rory and Garaith both agreed, although they seemed less invested in the win than Griff. He supposed that was the difference between them, the reason he was destined to lead, and they to follow. His father might believe that winning wasn't everything, but he was wrong. Griff was willing to do whatever it took to win, at any cost.

⚜

"Feast ready yet?" Griff asked as he came into the kitchen, seeing his mother standing at a fireplace taller than he was, basting a whole roasting pig on a spit. "I'm starvin'."

"You stink!" Sibyl wrinkled her freckled nose at her son as he bent to kiss the top of her head. "Go bathe in the stream with the rest of the men."

"Too cold," Griff complained. "Can I use yer spring?"

"Don't let your father catch you," Sibyl warned as Griff stole the apple from the pig's mouth, dodging his mother's swat.

"What?" He grinned, taking a big bite out of it. "I washed me hands!"

Griff grabbed an errant chair and pulled it up to the end of their long dining table. Beitrus, their old midwife, sat there kneading dough for bread. Moira, who ran the MacFalon castle almost singlehandedly, and had for years, sat with her, both of the old women chatting amiably. It had been poor old Beitrus who had offered to try Sibyl's "cure" for the wulver curse. She and Kirstin were the only two women who had ever taken the cure, and it had turned out to be quite permanent.

Sibyl had expressed her hope over the years that perhaps the effects would wear off and the women would be able to turn wolf again, but alas, that hadn't happened. Kirstin, who was married to The MacFalon now, didn't seem to mind. And old Beitrus said she was too old to turn wolf anymore anyway. She joked that the only thing turning wolf was good for at her age was better eyesight to sew by—and she didn't have hands to do that with in wulver form, so what use was it, after all? Besides, she often traveled back and forth between the MacFalon castle and the wulver den—she and Moira had become good friends and traded both recipes and herbal remedies—and while the Scots on MacFalon land had grown used to the wulvers over the past twenty years, it was still safer to remain human in their presence. Raife hadn't been joking, Griff knew, when he said they were the last of their kind, and most humans would kill them out of fear alone.

"I heard t'young girls talkin' 'bout yer sword skills in the Great Hunt today," Beitrus teased, pulling off a bit of dough and rolling it between her hands before putting it on a tray.

"They'd better not know anything about his sword skills," Sibyl called over her shoulder as she handed a young wulver girl—Colleen, a comely lass, Griff noted, who gave him a sly look—a stack full of wooden bowls so she could begin setting their places at the table. "Or they'll be scrubbing pots until their tails fall off."

Griff snickered, but he raised his eyebrows at Sibyl's sly smirk. "Aye? Is that so?"

"I heard ye got a scoldin' today, young pup." Moira stood, groaning softly as she put her hands at her lower back and arched. Griff just snorted at that, taking another noisy bite of apple. Moira gave him a sympathetic smile, leaning over to ruffle his hair. "He's hard on ye, but it's only a'cause he loves ye."

"Funny way of showin' it," Griff replied, mouth full.

"Ye'll understand why, some day," Beitrus told him, rolling another bit of dough in her hands. They were the very hands that had brought Griff into the world, which felt both comforting and strange at the same time as he watched her make biscuits. "Ye might even miss it."

"I doubt it." He rolled his eyes, ducking as his mother reached over to playfully smack him as she passed, finishing off his apple.

"You know, you're expected to lead them all, some day," Sibyl reminded him, stopping to press a soft kiss on his forehead instead of slapping him. She almost had to go on tiptoe to do it, even though she was standing and he was straddling a wooden chair.

"He'll ne'er let me lead," he growled, tossing the apple core into the fire—perfect aim. "Just like he doesn't even let us use real swords."

"Mayhaps yer destiny lies elsewhere," Moira mused, moving to help the younger wulver girls set the table on her end. Griff snorted at that, too. Talk of fate and destiny and prophecies bored him. He'd heard them his whole life, but they never really amounted to much. Just a lot of words in a book, written like code that they were supposed to translate.

"Moira..." Sibyl gave the old Scotswoman a dark glance, a clear warning. That caught Griff's attention.

"Aye, Mistress, aye," Moira muttered, eyes down as she set the table.

"Sibyl!" Laina poked her head in, glancing around at the crowded kitchen, wulver women bustling everywhere getting food ready for the feast. "Kirstin and Donal'd like t'see ye."

"Coming." Sibyl sighed, wiping her hands on her apron before untying it as she followed Laina out.

"What were ye sayin'?" Griff asked Moira as the woman came to take the tray, now filled with biscuits, from Beitrus. "'Bout m'destiny?"

"Oh ye've heard it all a'fore, lad." Moira gave him a half-smile as Maire, Griff's younger sister, took the tray from her hands, heading for the oven. "Y'know, t'prophecy of t'red wulver."

"Aye, t'red wulver, wit' t'red eyes." Griff rolled those same eyes as Maire came back carrying a tray laden with little pastries. "But what am I supposed to do? Whose savior am I again?"

"The future's uncertain." Moira sighed, leaning back and rubbing her tired eyes. "But there's somethin' to the prophecy, methinks. Even if it's the stuff of legend now."

"Ye're right t'question it, lad," Beitrus assured him with a pat of her hand on his arm. "The words're old and the translation isn't clear."

"Snitch!" Maire went to slap Griff's sneaky hand, but he was too quick for her. The pastries were juicy little bits filled with gravy and rabbit and he went to steal another one, but Maire gave him a dark look, sliding the tray down the table, out of his long reach.

"Brat." He scowled at his sister, wondering what in the world Rory saw in the girl. She was tall and dark-haired, like their father, and she had Sibyl's delicate features, but a wulver's blue eyes. She was comely enough, he supposed, but such a mouthy know-it-all, he didn't know how Rory

- 13 -

could possibly stand being around her for more than five minutes.

"Jus' a'cause ye won at swordplay doesn'a mean ye get served a'fore e'eryone else." Maire wrinkled her freckled nose at him—she had her mother's pale skin and tendency to burn instead of turn brown like most of the wulver women.

"That's exactly what it means." Griff grinned.

"Not just ye, y'arrogant arse," his sister snapped. "Ye weren't t'only one out there swingin' a wooden sword."

"Aye, but I was t'best one," Griff called as his sister went to get more food for the table. She flipped her long, black braid over her shoulder in a huff and he laughed, tuning back into the conversation between Beitrus and Moira.

"We can'na tell 'em a'fore we know," Beitrus cautioned, glancing toward the entrance to the kitchen, as if worried Sibyl might reappear. "'Tis too dangerous, unless we know fer sure."

"What else could it be?" Moira scoffed. "It says the lost packs can be found in the Temple of Asher and Ardis—and legend says the temple's hidden on Skara Brae."

"Skara Brae, hm?" Griff's eyebrows went up at that. "What lost packs? You mean—more wulvers? I thought we were the last."

The two old women exchanged a look, and then looked up at him as he stood, staring down at them.

"Are there more of us, then?" Griff prompted.

"We do'na know..." Beitrus shrugged one frail shoulder. "Mayhaps. The text is unclear."

"Oh, I think it's clear enough." Moira snorted.

"Lost packs," Griff mused. A sharp zing of excitement went through his body at the thought. He hadn't put much stock in prophecies and ancient wulver texts, but the idea that there were, mayhaps, other wulvers out there—now, that was interesting.

"Do'na tell yer mother I said anythin'," Beitrus hissed. "Sibyl's still mad, twenty years later, that I stole t'cure and swallowed it, jus' to test it."

"Do'na worry. I'll keep yer secrets." Griff gave the old woman a wink as he headed toward the secret entrance to the spring that led to his parents' quarters. It was a cool spring, but not nearly as cold as the creek up top.

His mother had been right about one thing—he did stink. Griff stripped off his clothes and jumped in, the shock of the water hitting him like a wall, but he reveled in it.

It would serve two purposes—cleaning his body and clearing his head. The former wasn't all that important, except that he intended to find a little wolf tail later—but the latter was paramount. He needed a clear head to make the right decision. And he had a feeling that the decision he was contemplating would be the biggest decision he might ever make in his entire life.

❧

Griff was up before first light. He had one candle lit to dress by. As the pack leader's son, he had the privilege of having his own room, even though the den was growing ever more crowded. In his bed, a young wulver woman— her name was Colleen, a shapely little lass who had offered her bottom up to him more than once the night before— rolled over and sighed in her sleep. She'd be surprised when she woke and found him gone. They both would—the other girl, Eryn, was curled up at the foot of the bed, in wolf form. Her white paws twitched in her sleep, like she was dreaming about running.

Griff thought of his mother as he rolled up the map of a route to Skara Brae he'd pinched from his father's room. Skara Brae was an island in the far north of Scotland, and it would be a long trip. Mayhaps even a treacherous one, given the number of reavers that roamed far beyond the borderlands now. But a necessary one. His decision had been made with a clear head. He would go to Skara Brae and find the lost packs. If there were other packs out there, mayhaps they were leaderless. Mayhaps he wouldn't have to challenge his father's position. Mayhaps that silly prophecy would serve a purpose after all.

Griff blew out the candle and slipped out of his room into the dark tunnel. His parents were likely still sleeping in the room beside his. The den was quiet, resting. Griff turned and headed toward the long staircase that would lead to the surface, where he would go to the barn and saddle his horse for travel. But before he reached the stairway, he stopped at the pack meeting hall, looking at the round table where his father always sat with the rest of the wulver council. His seat was to his father's left, Darrow's to his right. There was no head of the table, but everyone knew who was alpha.

Griff slipped his dirk out and stuck it into the wooden table in front of his seat. It was an old wulver way to mark your territory—it would let everyone know he'd be back, and that anyone who wanted his spot would be challenging him. Then he shouldered his pack and left the den of his childhood behind him.

Chapter Two

"I'm goin' t'win this time!" Bridget's sword glinted in the sun, and she had a brief hope that, just for a moment, it had distracted Alaric enough for her to triumph and turn her bold statement into truth.

But Alaric wasn't one to ever let her win, and while she was good—one of the best students he'd ever trained, as he often told her—she still had only bested him a few times.

His claymore was far bigger and heavier than her long sword, but he wielded it with frightening accuracy. Bridget went forward and back, her feminine form an advantage in the way she moved, with the grace of a dancer, but her footwork was wasted on a fighter like Alaric. He moved with the efficiency of a warrior, expending energy only when necessary, and despite his massive size, he was always ahead of her in some way. His claymore went left, and so did Bridget's long sword, but at the last moment, the big man's weapon changed direction, a feat which took a tremendous amount of strength.

She had always been vulnerable to fakes and feints, a fact Alaric used to his advantage.

"No!" Bridget brought her sword back just in time to block the blow. She panted with the effort it took to hold him at bay, but it didn't last long. Alaric saw her weakness and exploited it, unending her smaller form and sprawling her in the dirt. He pointed his claymore at her throat, although the tip stayed several feet away.

"Ye're dead." Alaric shook his head regretfully, as if he was truly sorry he'd "killed" her. "Ye lemme fake y'out again. Will ye e'er learn?"

"I did'na fall fer it t'first two times!" she reminded him, berating herself internally for falling for it the last time, or at all. Why did she always trust that someone was going to do what they looked like they were going to do?

"Ye know I've ne'er trained or fought a better student." He sheathed his claymore and held a hand out to help her up.

Bridget took it with a sigh, letting him pull her easily off the ground, even wearing mostly English armor, at least on her upper body. She brushed off her plaid. Her tailbone ached where she'd landed on it, but her pride was far more hurt. It wasn't losing that bothered her—losing was part of learning—it was making the same mistakes over and over that irked her.

"Yer doin' well, lass." Alaric's hand fell to her shoulder, as big as a ham, squeezing gently. "A fine guardian-in-trainin'. An' I know yer mother agrees wit' me, a fine handmaiden-in-training as well."

"Thank ye." She gave him an encouraged smile. Praise from Alaric wasn't earned easily, nor did she take it lightly.

"Jus' watch yer hips'n'torso. They ne'er lie." His left hand moved quickly, fingers snapping beside her ear, and her head turned left, instinctive. That's when he slapped her cheek lightly with his right. "D'ye see where me body was turned?"

He pointed to his chest and then left, dropping her a wink. "It gave me away, aye?"

"I'm too distractible." She sighed, sheathing her long sword, both cheeks burning, even though he'd only slapped one.

"Go t'yer mother by da pool, Miss Distractible." Alaric smiled. "It's time fer t'purification."

Bridget took off running—as fast as she could run with a sword sheathed at her side. Before she entered the temple proper, the sword came off, and she switched roles as quickly as she shed her armor. Alaric would yell at her for leaving it near the entrance, but she was already running late and her mother would be waiting.

She wore two temple hats, as both guardian-in-training and priestess-in-training, and learning both roles took most of her day. She didn't have a lot of free time, which seemed strange, given there were no other people in the temple, aside from Alaric and Aleesa. But it had always been that way, since she'd been abandoned at the temple entrance as an infant and the couple she knew as mother and father had taken her in. She really didn't know anything else.

Bridget stopped to quickly change from her plaid to her temple robe just outside the cave, taking the headpiece with the three-goddesses on it and placing it in the midst of her still-sweaty red hair.

"N'runnin', Bridget," her mother called with a sigh.

Aleesa was already kneeling at the pool when Bridget rushed in. She slowed almost immediately, still breathing hard. The pool was in the middle of a large cave with a tall, domed ceiling that had a central opening. It shone down into the pool below, and even at night, in the darkness, with almost no light in the sky, a beam of sun or moon focused in the pond. Alaric said it was due to some sort of reflective metal that had been embedded into the stone high above.

Bridget's heartbeat returned to some semblance of normal as she knelt opposite her mother, meeting Aleesa's soft, knowing eyes over the surface of the pool. Bridget's face flushed and she knew her mother understood exactly where she'd been, and why she was late. Could she help it that she liked training to be a guardian a little more than she liked training to be a temple priestess?

Not that she didn't love the sacred feel of the pool, how it calmed her soul. Just being amidst the stone monoliths that surrounded the little body of water in the cave helped ground and still her. Feeling the earth under her bare feet, looking at the beam of light shining into the center of the pool, gave her a sense of peace she didn't find anywhere else. She knew that the way the light fell, in relation to the stones, could be used to find and make many time and season calculations. She was in the process of learning the many ways these were related to both astronomy and astrology, starting to calculate these things as Aleesa taught her more and more.

But even if she hadn't been a priestess-in-training, she knew this place would feel like home to her.

"Are ye ready?" Aleesa cocked her head in question and Bridget took a deep breath, giving her a slow nod.

There was already a bowl in front of her filled with water and fragrant herbs and Bridget leaned over it, seeing a brief glimpse of her reflection—big eyes, mussed hair—as she picked the bowl up in both hands, breathing in the scent. The women worked together, perfectly in sync—they'd done this hundreds of times, since Bridget was very young—Alessa calling out the ancient words, Bridget responding in kind, as they dipped their fingers into the water, tracing patterns. Then, they took fingers full of the herbs, whispering the words in sync as they tossed them into the pool, kissing the side of the bowl before each pass. The whole cave smelled like silvermoon and heather. It was heady and made Bridget smile.

The bowls were then set aside, and each woman raised a ritual sword, incanting words together, the energy between them rising like a tide, their swords held out over the water. The ritual swords were far lighter than Bridget's practice one and were the only weapons allowed in the temple proper. Their voices melded together, almost a song, the rhythmic chant they spoke together, ancient Gaelic words, filling the cavern.

The prayer they spoke together was filled with power. Both women knew it, felt it. Bridget felt the hilt of the sword grow warm, as it always did, before the sword flared with flame. The first time it had happened, she'd nearly dropped it into the pool, even though Aleesa had warned her it would happen. She hadn't quite believed it, even though she'd lived in the temple her whole life and had seen the ritual performed.

As the prayer came to an end, the fire changed from a normal orange glow to silver. That was the time they slowly lowered their swords into the pool, extinguishing the flames with a low hissing sound. Steam rose up from the pool toward the domed roof of the cave. Bridget was always a little sad at the end of the ritual, but when she looked up and saw her mother's frown, her gaze fell immediately to the water.

"A single warrior approaches." Aleesa's eyes focused on the image reflected in the pool, widening in surprise. The pool served many purposes, and sometimes divination was one of them. "Ye mus' go out t'meet 'im, Bridget."

Bridget felt her mouth go dry. She'd only ever gone out to the crossroads once before to meet someone seeking entrance to the Temple of Asher and Ardis, and in that case, the man had not been worthy. Just someone seeking the riches of the temple—which were the stuff of legend, but not real. The only value within the temple was the magic it contained within its sacred walls, nothing payable in gold or silver, which is what most people seemed to want. Bridget hadn't even gotten to the point of challenging the old man—she'd simply sent him on his way. The entrance to the temple was hidden, and she was quite safe during the inquiry.

"Hurry! Go!" Aleesa urged her daughter, waving her away, and that got Bridget moving.

Her plaid was waiting, and she put that on instead of her temple robe, which she left on the floor as she rushed out to retrieve her armor. Aleesa would cluck and frown about her messiness, but under the circumstances, she knew she wouldn't be in too much trouble for not cleaning up after herself.

Alaric was standing at the temple entrance as she approached and she glanced guiltily down at her armor on the dirt floor. He frowned at it, then looked up at her, disappointment on his face, but that changed when their eyes met.

"Someone approaches?" he asked, eyes wide in surprise.

"Aye, a warrior." She nodded, wondering if her fear showed. She hoped not. "Mother said I mus' go out and meet 'im."

Alaric gave a nod, already picking up her gear and helping her dress. Getting out of the stuff by herself was possible, but getting it on was much more difficult. They approached the secret entrance together. Alaric had been the one to do this before her, but he'd been training her over the years, and had deemed her ready. And if he thought she was ready, then it had to be so. Even if she was, at times, still susceptible to feints. Her challenger wouldn't know that, would he? Alaric was one of the best fighters in the world, and he'd trained her—so if she could keep up with Alaric...

She'd have to trust that all would be as it should be.

That's what she told herself as Alaric opened the underground passage that would lead her to the rock outcropping at the crossroads. She felt his hand on her shoulder, a sudden weight, and glanced back.

"Yer a fine guardian, lass," he assured her. "It'll all be as it should."

Funny that she'd just spoken those words to herself. She gave him a nod, stepping out into the light of day. It was a glorious summer day and it made her wonder what normal maidens her age were doing. Picking flowers and making daisy chains, mayhaps? But not Bridget. She was walking out in full armor to meet a challenging warrior. Alaric and Alessa often said those words, "All will be as it should," but sometimes, she wondered. Had she been meant to be abandoned at the temple? Meant to be trained as the priestess and guardian of the Temple of Ardis and Asher? It seemed a strange charge for a human girl who lived with and had been parented by wulvers, especially given that the legend of Ardis and Asher was a wulver legend and not a human one.

But she was doing it, standing behind the remote outcropping where she could disappear to safety inside the temple again, if she needed to. If the warrior sought healing and knew of the temple, the guardian had to yield and bring him inside. She had only glimpsed his image briefly in the pool, a big man on horseback wearing a Scots plaid and gear but no armor, not even chainmail or a helmet. Mayhaps he sought healing only?

Her armor was more English than Scottish, to be honest, made for a knight, with a breastplate and a full helmet and faceplate, although she had the freedom of her legs being bare—a Scot couldn't be tied down, that's what Alaric always said.

She was glad of the helmet, though, because it hid her face. She had learned, long ago, to disguise her voice, and had practiced throwing it beyond the outcropping into the crossroads, a booming reply to the inquiry of a seeker. There was a small, reflective piece of metal positioned so she could see the warrior's approach, although he could not see her or discern her position.

Bridget had a moment to just study him as he slowed his horse. She lifted her faceplate so she could do so more clearly. The war horse turned in easy, slow circles as the big man looked around, taking in his barren surroundings. The rocks were the only thing of interest, of course, as it was meant to be. The dark-haired warrior squinted at the rocks, brow lowered, mouth drawn down into a frown.

"Uri, this is ridiculous," the man muttered, patting his horse's neck. "'Ere goes nothin'."

The man sat back up, running a hand through his thick, dark hair. He was young, but not a boy. Mayhaps her age, she thought, cocking her head and staring at him. A considerable opponent to be sure. She really hoped he was here for healing, because she didn't want to have to fight him. She would, if she had to—but if she could just bid him enter, that would be better.

"I seek entrance t'the Temple of Asher'n'Ardis!" The man's voice carried to her easily. It was a pleasant sound, and she sensed no fear in it. No evil either. Just a little annoyance and impatience. This was a man who was used to gaining entry, wherever he went. That much was clear. Not royalty though. Not that kind of entitlement. She sensed more of a... confidence about him. Mayhaps a little arrogance?

Bridget swallowed, lubricating her throat, before lowering her voice and booming her own reply, "Who seeks entrance?"

The horse startled, giving a low whinny and pawing the dirt. The man handled the horse with ease, turning the animal toward the rocks.

"Now we're gettin' somewhere," he muttered, calling back, "My name's Griffith."

Just Griffith? No surname? No title? She cocked her head, frowning at that. A simple man, then? But he did not look simple. The man was big, well-muscled. This man trained, and he trained hard.

"An' what d'ye seek, Griffith?" Bridget called, making sure she kept her voice an octave lower than usual. Funny, how his name felt in her mouth. Familiar, somehow, although she'd never heard it called.

"Knowledge."

Her heart sank. Not healing, then. A seeker who was true, who sought anything other than healing, would have to force the guardian to yield in combat if they wanted entrance. The guardian could, on rare occasion, choose to yield without a fight, but it hardly ever happened. Had never happened, in her lifetime, or Alaric's either, he'd told her.

"Are ye there?" Griff called. Impatient. She'd have to remember that.

She wasn't relishing fighting this man, who was twice her size at least. Were Alaric and Aleesa watching in the pool? They would be, of course. It would be her first real combat with an entrant, and she didn't want to disappoint her father. Especially after her loss to him that afternoon.

"Ye mus' prove yerself worthy, seeker," she called, managing to keep the tremble from her voice. It was both excitement, and, mayhaps, a little fear. "By bestin' me in combat."

"Then come out an' meet me, stranger." Griff straightened in his saddle, a slow smile spreading across his face.

"I'm t'guardian of t'temple." Bridget stepped toward the rocks, putting her face plate down, and her hand on the hilt of her sword. "And ye shall not pass 'til ye best me an'force me t'yield."

"I can'na best ye unless I can see ye." Griff stared at the rocks, blinking in surprise when Bridget appeared from behind them. She'd never used the secret entrance before, but it worked just like Alaric said it would.

"I can'na fight a boy." Griff snorted as he slid off his horse. She saw him searching the rocks with his eyes, wondering where in the world she'd come from. "T'would nuh be right."

"I'm not a boy." Bridget raised her sword, feeling anger burning in her chest at the man's words. A boy, indeed! Not only wasn't she a boy—and what a surprise he'd get when he was bested by a girl!—she was a warrior, trained by one of the best warriors in all of Scotland.

She might not have been quite good enough to beat Alaric, but she could beat this man—even if he was twice her size.

"I do'na wanna fight ye, lad." Griff sighed, shaking his head as he unsheathed his sword.

"Ye've no choice, seeker." Bridget straightened her spine to give herself full height, but the top of her head still barely reached his shoulder. "If ye wan' entry t'the temple, ye mus' force t'guardian t'yield."

"I do'na hafta kill ye?" Griff frowned. "I'd hate t'hafta kill ye."

"Tis not to the death." Bridget rolled her eyes behind her face plate. "But ye'll be lucky if I do'na kill *ye,* seeker."

"Let's get this over wit', lad." Griff stepped away from his horse with another deep sigh, moving quickly into fighting stance, sword up.

"I'm not a lad!" she snapped gruffly as she swung, their swords clashing with the ring of steel in the afternoon sunlight.

She was still a little tired, muscles sore, from her training with Alaric, but she wasn't going to let that stop her. The big man blocked her blow easily, taking a graceful step back and sighing again, like it was quite taxing to be forced to fight her. Bridget felt anger rising and tried to swallow it down. Her father had trained her to stay calm and cool-headed in a fight and normally, she didn't have any problem with that. But for some reason, seeing this giant, broad-shouldered man smirking, even chuckling as she advanced, made her furious.

Griff's sword blocked another one of her blows and Bridget swung again, more quickly this time, driving him backward. The horse pawed the ground a few feet away, as if objecting to his master's sudden predicament. It didn't take Bridget long to push the big man back toward the other side of the crossroads, going after him relentlessly, swing after swing of her heavy long sword.

"Well, lad, ye take yer job seriously, that much is clear." Griff panted as he rallied, getting his bearings and whirling on her, his sword blow coming so hard and fast, it actually knocked her off her feet.

Her pride was hurt more than her bottom as she struggled to stand.

"Ye'll right, lad?" Griff frowned, reaching down a hand to help her up, and that's when something inside Bridget snapped.

She was up in an instant, running at him like a bull, her helmet hitting him hard in the gut. She heard the air go out of him and he grunted. Her fast action had surprised him, caught him off guard, and he stumbled. Unfortunately, he didn't go down as she planned. It took him just two strides to regain his footing and he gave a low growl, whirling on her, sword at the ready.

"I'm endin' this now." Griff snarled, coming at her so fast and furious, she could barely see his sword flashing. She had to repel him only on instinct, which she managed, but it took her breath away. "Someone needs t'teach ye a lesson."

Bridget winced as the big man's sword slid against hers and she found herself pinned against the rock—how they'd managed to get so far, she didn't know. He crushed her against the stone with his weight until she couldn't breathe at all, even in her armor. Her breastplate dug into her skin, compressing the air from her lungs. She tried to move, but there was no possible way. He covered her completely, his arm across her chest and shoulders, heavy as a log, his thigh between hers, so thick it felt like she was straddling a tree.

Bridget struggled, trying to lift her sword, but he had that trapped too, with the heavy weight of his boot. The anger rising in her blurred her vision. She could only see a slit of him through her face plate. His breath was hot and heavy, but not unpleasant. He ducked his head so he could see her eyes—his were the strangest color she'd ever seen, a sort of amber, and for a moment, she was transfixed. The man searched her eyes with his, far too much amusement in them at having bested her, but there was an empathy there too, that bothered her even more.

He let up just a little as he asked, voice soft, "D'ye yield?"

Bridget thought of Alaric, watching her in the clear surface of the scrying pool—or mayhaps he was standing even now on the other side of the rock wall, watching via the reflective metal she'd used to spy on the approaching warrior. She wouldn't yield—couldn't let him down.

She shook her head, glaring at him, and wheezed, "No."

"Yield, lad," he said gently. "I *will* best ye, and if ye yield now, t'will mean far less bruisin' fer ye—an' yer pride."

Bridget snarled, throwing all her weight at him—not that it made that much of a difference. How could Alaric have handed over this task to her? How could he have believed she could best someone twice her size? But he had charged her with this task. He believed in her. He thought she could do this, had trained her to be better than this.

"Get off me, ye fat oaf," she snapped, hearing him chuckle, then sigh and shake his head as he eased back.

"So ye yield then?"

"No!" She grunted, bringing her knee up between his— it wasn't exactly fair, but she knew it would work. Luckily the man was a Scot, and like her, he wore a plaid to keep his legs free for running and climbing. She'd accidentally kneed Alaric this way on a few occasions and had completely incapacitated him for a while.

But the big man was too fast. He stepped back, just barely avoiding the knee to his crotch. That gave her the opportunity to go after him again, and she did, with everything she had. They danced and swung, metal clashing. It was exhausting, but Bridget didn't give up. This smug man wasn't going to enter her temple, not if she could prevent it. He wasn't worthy.

"Yield!" Bridget yelled, swinging her sword hard over her head at the dark-haired beast but he blocked her blow. She was satisfied to see the surprise in his eyes, though, at her onslaught.

It was that brief moment of patting herself on the back that was her undoing. That and the feint he made, untangling his sword from hers and jabbing at her. The sword went under her arm and Bridget took an instinctive step back, but it was too late.

He used his sword as a lever, pushing her forward, toward him. Their bodies jarred together and Bridget felt her teeth rattle in her head. Running into the man's chest was like running into a stone wall. She gasped, all her breath gone from her lungs as the man tripped her, hooking a foot around her calf and tipping her into the dirt.

"Yer finished, lad." Griff planted his sword in the dirt right beside her head and Bridget winced. "Now, take me t'the temple, a'fore I really hafta hurt ye."

"Aye." She swallowed her pride, along with a cloud full of dust, struggling to stand. She ignored the hand the man offered, making her way slowly to her feet and trying to find her balance. She leaned against the outcropping, ashamed that Alaric would be seeing this. "O'er there. See t'rock?"

Her voice was hoarse.

"Aye." Griff gave a brief nod, lifting a hand to shade his eyes in the afternoon sun.

"We'll meet ye by t'rock." She waved him on, limping toward the secret entrance.

"We?" The big man frowned. "Were d'ya think yer goin', lad? I did'na come all this way t—"

To lick my wounds.

A hand grabbed her elbow and she shook it off, snarling.

"Let go'a me!"

"Are ye hurt?" Griff asked, concerned. She bristled at his tone. It only made the hurt, real and imagined, worse.

"T'rock!" she snapped, pointing. "Go!"

"I'm n'accustomed t'taking orders from boys," the man snorted, and the arrogance in his voice broke her.

"I'm not a boy!" she snapped again, whirling toward him and flipping her faceplate up to glare at him. He stared at her for a moment, confused, as if trying to figure something out.

She could still scarce breathe and, in one swift motion, pulled her helmet off her head, letting her long, auburn hair spill like a rain of fire over the silver breastplate.

The look on his face was priceless.

His mouth dropped open, his strange-colored eyes going wide.

"Yer a lass?" he choked, blinking fast.

"Aye." She stared at him, drawing herself up as tall as she could, pointing again to the rock where Alaric would take the man and his horse into the temple. "Ye bested a woman. I hope yer proud o'yerself. Now, if ye wanna enter the temple, I suggest ye go t'the rock."

She didn't bother to stay and see what he would do. Bridget went straight to the secret entrance in the rock outcropping and slipped inside. She managed to walk upright, in a straight line, until she was out of his sight line.

Only then did she allow the tears that threatened to flow, and she went to her knees, sword and helmet forgotten in the grass, as she wept like she hadn't since she was a little girl.

Chapter Three

Griff stood at the rock face feeling like a complete fool. Not only had he just nearly killed a woman—what kind of temple used a woman dressed in armor as a guardian anyway?—but now he'd walked Uri down the road to yet another rock, and he stood waiting for someone to appear and allow him entrance to a place that, up until half an hour ago, he wasn't quite sure actually existed. Mayhaps it was all a ruse, he thought, glowering at the rock. It was almost as tall as he was and he saw no door, no way in or out of any temple.

Of course, the guardian—*the woman*, his mind corrected, and he felt another twinge of guilt at what he'd done—had appeared out of nowhere, or so it seemed. Mayhaps this rock was the same. Or mayhaps they were all just bandits, a ring of reavers working together with the pirates who had given him passage and had told him where to go, how to find his way to this strange island, to this particular crossroads and rock outcropping. Mayhaps the woman was just a distraction, and even now, there were men hidden somewhere with arrows pointed at his head.

Although if they were hidden somewhere, he didn't know where.

There were no trees on these rolling green hills, nothing from here until the sea.

Griff lifted his nose and sniffed the air, but caught nothing except the scent of his horse, the salt of the sea, and the green of the grass mixed with a carpet of heather. And the woman. He scented her still, something he'd noticed during their encounter, but had dismissed. He'd thought it was just the smell of a youngster, a pup. He'd realized the smaller figure in armor was just a lad right off, but why hadn't he realized she was a woman? He chastised himself again, squinting at the sun overhead, remembering the way she'd pulled off her helmet, the fire that flashed in her grey-green eyes.

He'd been more than surprised, truth be told. The lad—the figure in armor he was sure was just a young boy—had put up a good fight. He... er, *she*... had been taught well. If she'd been comparable in size, mayhaps she would have stood a chance. He'd started to feel a little bad for her, before he found out she was actually a girl. Now... he wasn't sure what he felt. Whatever it was, it was strange. He'd felt something when he first met her eyes, just peering into the slit in her faceplate.

But when she'd yanked off her helmet and glared at him, and he watched a cascade of red fire roll over her shoulders, it hit him with the force of a herd of horses. It had literally taken his breath away. At first, he thought it was just the fact that she was a woman, that he had spilled a woman into the dirt and threatened her bodily harm. But it wasn't just that. There was something else, something about her. He wondered if she'd felt it, too.

Then he remembered the way she'd glared at him, how her spine had straightened, her pride clearly bruised, maybe even more than her body, and chuckled to himself.

He was so lost in thought, he almost didn't see it happen.

Griff frowned, seeing the rock move out of the corner of his eye, an effect that startled his horse. Uri whinnied and stepped sideways, shaking his head, and Griff grabbed hold of his reins to keep the big animal from bolting.

"Ye've bested our guardian, and so've earned entrance t'the Temple of Asher'n'Ardis." The voice made Griff whirl around and he stared at the man who stood at the cave entrance. It had been quite hidden by the rock, and Griff frowned, wondering how the man had moved the giant thing. "Follow me."

"M'horse," Griff said, but the man was already moving back underground, into the cave.

"Bring 'im," the man called over his shoulder.

Griff urged Uri forward, but the horse fought him. The animal didn't like the idea of going underground, not knowing what was down there in the dark, and Griff didn't blame him. But he hadn't traveled all this way to stop now. He tugged the horse's reins, making a gruff noise in his throat, and Uri reluctantly followed.

"Is the... uh..." Griff realized he didn't know the woman's name. "The lass... the guardian... is she hurt?"

The man snorted. "Only 'er pride."

Griff grinned at that. "I did'na know she was a lass."

"She'll be glad t'hear it." The man stopped, pressing something on the wall, and behind them, the rock moved again, blocking out the light.

Griff glanced back, checking to make sure his sword was still in his sheath, just in case. The other man lit a fire in a bowl, mumbling something, a prayer perhaps. Griff sighed with impatience. He'd traveled a long way to find this place, and he had a lot of questions he hoped someone here had the answers to.

The fire bowl lit the underground cavern. This place would provide protection, Griff realized, from both the weather and the sea. And, of course, enemies. Much like their den at home, he thought, studying the big man who turned back toward him, the fire lighting his lined face.

The man was as tall as Griff, steel gray hair falling to his shoulders, a thick beard covering his face. It was only when he turned toward him and Griff caught his scent that they recognized each other—not as men who knew each other, but as wulvers.

"Yer like me." Griff blinked at the man, incredulous.

He'd never seen another wulver outside of his own den.

"Aye." The man wrinkled his nose, almost a snarl—it was a gesture Griff was used to. The man was scenting him. "Ye've come a long way, lad."

"Aye," he agreed. "I seek answers."

"C'mon, then."

The big man led him further into the cavern, and Griff pulled his horse along. They came to a turn, and the man led him left, showing him a place where he could tie Uri in a stall and leave him beside two other horses.

"D'ye 'ave anyone t'tend him?" Griff asked, glancing around the cavern.

"I'm 'fraid not." The old man shook his head. "There're jus' a few of us."

"Can ye wait fer me t'do so?"

"Aye."

Griff took the time to rub the horse down. The animal hadn't liked traveling on the ship he'd taken to the island. It had been quite an adventure so far, for both of them. There were two other horses in the stalls, fine looking animals, and Griff admired them. He gave Uri a feed bag and tossed straw down for him before following the other man through the tunnels of the cavern.

"Where'd ye hear 'bout our temple?" The man held the fire bowl aloft as he walked, far too slow for Griff, but he accommodated the man's pace. The other wulver was an older man, but by no means ancient. Griff guessed that he was mayhaps twenty years older than Griff's own father.

"The healers in m'den." Griff followed the man around a corner, light coming from the end of the tunnel.

"Leave yer weapons 'ere." The older man unsheathed a sword, leaving it on a rack built into the cavern wall, glancing back at Griff, who did the same. "No weapons're allowed in t'sanctuary. Ye may 'ave it back when ye go."

"But weapons're required t'enter?" Griff's brows went up, and he smirked.

"Nuh, n'required." The man balanced the fire bowl in his hands as he walked. They were entering the main part of the temple, exiting the cavernous tunnels. "Those who seek healin' here, receive it wit'out challenge. But ye're not in need of such healin'. Ye're seekin' somethin' else."

That much was true. Griff didn't know how the man knew. But mayhaps it was just a guess, and he knew nothing. How could he? Griff himself had only a vague idea of what it was he sought here in the temple of his ancestors. The lost packs. Mayhaps there was something he was meant to do, some greater destiny out there in the world for him, but whatever it was, there were wulvers out there who needed a leader.

The lost packs that Beitrus and Moira had spoken of must be part of whatever destiny awaited him. He was almost certain of that fact. To his knowledge, there was no other place where he could find out about the lost packs except for this fabled temple. Now he knew it was not the stuff of legend, but it actually existed. That was, at least, a step in the right direction.

The older man led him into a large, cavernous room. It was warm and inviting and felt very much like back home in his den. He didn't wonder at it too much—they were, after all, underground, and that's where all wulver dens were located, and for good reason. He supposed it shouldn't have been a surprise that the Temple of Asher and Ardis, the first wulvers, was also underground.

"Ye've bested our Guardian, seeker," the older man told him, as they neared the light at the end of the tunnel. "Ye're welcome in the Temple of Ardis'n'Asher, the first wulvers, and as Guardian meself, I'll do what I can t'help ye find what ye seek. Our temple priestess, Aleesa, is also at yer disposal, seeker."

"Thank ye." Griff looked up as they stepped into the warm, inviting room. There was a fireplace on one wall, with a fire lit in it. The smell of roasting meat made his stomach rumble. It reminded him of their big kitchen back home, in miniscule version.

The older man put the fire bowl in the middle of a wooden table. Griff looked at the bowl closely for the first time. He could not see how or what was burning in it. It was too close to magic for his comfort.

"Is this our seeker, then?" A woman, older as well, with long, dark, plaited hair shot with streaks of gray, entered the room from the other side. She smiled at Griff in welcome, holding out her hands to him as she approached. She was still a stunningly beautiful woman, with full, red lips, a curvy, voluptuous figure under her priestess robe, and a smile that lit up the entire room. "I'm Aleesa, the high priestess of t'temple."

"M'name's Griff." He took both of her outstretched hands in his, raising one of them to his lips to kiss it. "And I'm, indeed, a seeker. I do hope that yer other temple guardian's doin' a'righ'?"

"Bridget?" Aleesa glanced over her shoulder at the entrance she had come through. "She's a tough 'un."

"I told 'im 'er pride's bruised more'n 'er body." The older man chuckled. Aleesa gave him a knowing smile.

"So ye're wulver as well?" Griff asked Aleesa as she bade him to sit down at the table where the fire bowl still burned.

"Aye, a'course." Aleesa waved the older man into a seat beside her. "What else did y'expect at the Temple of Asher'n'Ardis?"

"I s'pose." Griff gave a rueful laugh. "I've jus' ne'er known any other wulvers outside of m'own den. I did'na know any others existed."

"But ye clearly do'na believe that." The older man raised his craggy eyebrows. "Ye're here seekin' others."

"How d'ye know that?" Griff's own eyebrows rose in surprise. "I've n'spoken of that which I seek."

"We see much." Aleesa folded her hands in her lap and looked at Griff expectantly. "But we'd hear yer request. And as guardian and priestess of the temple, we'll do our best t'accommodate ye."

"I hafta tell ye, I do'na b'lieve in magic." Griff bristled at the smile the dark-haired woman gave him when he said this. To Griff, things beyond comprehension only seemed unexplainable. Like his uncle, Darrow, he was very much a skeptic when it came to magic spells and potions.

Granted, he knew his own mother, Sibyl, had concocted the "cure" for the wulver woman's monthly curse, and at least two wulver women, Beitrus and Kirstin, had taken that "cure," and both of them seemed unable to change to wolf form now, but Griff still had his doubts. Even as he looked into the flame of the bowl burning in front of him, he doubted.

Even seeing wasn't always believing.

He remembered the way the armored guardian had appeared from the rock outcropping, and wondered how such an illusion had been accomplished. But he still didn't believe it was magic. Tricks, certainly. Those were commonplace and could be explained. He had lived with healers his whole life, women many would call witches, but he knew their "magic" had far more to do with the natural world than anything beyond it.

Remembering the guardian, the woman who had revealed herself to him in one glorious unveiling, he glanced around the room, wondering why this pair of temple guardians would have allowed her to go out and meet him, instead of sending the bigger, older man out to fight.

Certainly, the man was no longer a young pup, but he was a man, and a wulver, which Griff was sure the young redhead was not. The man and woman at the table with him were wulvers—he could smell it on them. The man was, like Griff, a wulver warrior. He could transform into half-man, half-wolf, at his choosing.

Griff didn't know why it bothered him so much—mayhaps it was because the woman had nearly bested him, twice—but the thought of this man, old enough to be the young redhead's father, mayhaps even grandfather, waiting underground while she faced danger...

"It matters not what ye b'lieve." Aleesa glanced over Griff's shoulder, smiling in welcome. "Here's our Bridget now."

Griff could smell her.

She filled his senses, even before he turned his head to look at the woman who approached. Without her armor to hide her figure, Bridget was all woman. Her priestess robes, cinched at the waist, surprised him. They were just like the other woman, Aleesa's, made of some shiny, reflective white material that clung to her generous curves, a sight that made Griff salivate like a starving man who had just come upon a king's feast. Bridget nodded to the older couple, glancing briefly at Griff as she went about gathering cups and warming water over the fireplace.

"I hope ye're n'hurt, lass," Griff called to the redhead, seeing the way her back stiffened at his words. She continued to pour water, now warm, into four mugs. But she didn't reply. Griff looked at the man, whose name he still did not know, and felt a flash of anger. "What sorta man sends a young woman out t'do 'is work?"

"One who wants 'er t'learn," the old man replied simply. He met Griff's dark stare with his own. The older man's eyes were wulver blue, as were the woman's. He wondered where the red-haired, green-eyed creature bringing tea to them at the wooden table had come from. She was not a wulver, but she was like no human woman he had ever known. He certainly knew no women who donned armor and wielded swords, and then changed into silky priestess robes and murmured niceties as she sat beside him at the table.

"It is as it should be, father." Bridget sighed, lifting the mug toward her mouth, blowing on the hot liquid. Griff cocked his head, looking at her, at the pucker of her lips, the way her eyes lifted to meet his own. The way she looked at him filled him with heat. He shifted in his chair, looking up at Aleesa as she stood.

"I imagine ye're hungry, warrior." Aleesa nudged the younger woman and Bridget put down her mug, getting up to help set the table.

Griff offered to help, something he would never do at home, but the women waved him off, so he and the older man sat together at the table, face-to-face, while Griff wondered where to start.

As if reading his mind, the older man half-smiled, and asked, "What is't that ye seek, wulver warrior?"

Griff frowned into his mug of tea, a mug that seemed giant in the redhead's hands, but diminutive in his own. He supposed there was no better way than to just come out and say it.

"I need t'know where t'find the lost packs'o'wulvers."

Bridget, who had been reaching over his shoulder to place a wooden plate and spoon in front of him, stopped what she was doing to stare at him.

"And why d'ye seek this knowledge?" the gray-haired wulver asked.

"He's a wulver?" Bridget blurted, blinking at Griff in surprise. "Is e'eryone beyond these temple walls half-wolf'n'half-man? Am I t'only one who can'na change t'animal form?"

"A'course not." Aleesa smiled, putting the roast meat and a pot of vegetables on the table. "In fact, t'opposite's true. Most beasts who roam this world are either man or animal, not both."

"Tis true," Griff agreed, giving a laugh. The redhead glared at him as if finding out he was a wulver was the last insult she could possibly bear. "'Ave ye ne'er been beyond these temple walls?"

"A'course I have," Bridget snapped, pulling back, away from the brush of Griff's upper arm as if she had been burned. The silk of her robe brushing his skin was intoxicating. "Jus' not... far."

"'Bout as far as t'rocks ye met me at, I'd wager." Griff grinned.

"Ye'd n'lose that wager, lad." The older man chuckled and the redhead's spine stiffened again, her lips pursing prettily.

The old man looked at his daughter—Griff still couldn't quite comprehend how the young woman called the old wulver father, when clearly she was not their issue—smiling ruefully. "I can'na take 'er much further than I a'ready 'ave. She's been a fine student, an obedient daughter, an' her mother an' I love 'er dearly. We've trained 'er all these years t'fill two roles—that of temple handmaiden and temple guardian. Tis a heavy burden fer one so young, but there's no other. And 'er mother an' I'll n'live fore'er. Certainly, we'll live longer than most in the safety of this sacred place, and t'will keep us 'ere t'tend it 'til there's another."

"Tis as it should be, Father," Bridget reminded him, putting a pitcher of cool water in the middle of the table as she sat beside Griff.

"I wondered why ye'd send a woman out as temple guardian," Griff mused, accepting a delicious smelling leg of chicken with an empty plate as Aleesa carved. "But clearly ye've no other choice."

"I almos' bested ye—twice," Bridget reminded coolly. She plucked two errant feathers from the wing of a chicken on her plate with a vengeance.

"I mus' confess, I almos' let ye win." Griff grinned when she gave him a look, eyes narrowed to gray-green slits, like a cat. "But I've traveled a long way, seekin' knowledge at this temple. If I had t'kill ye, I s'pose I would've. A'fore I knew ye were a woman…"

"What's that hafta do wit' anythin'?" Bridget wrinkled her snub nose at him, reaching for her mug of tea. "I'm jus' as much a warrior as ye're. Me father was ona t'greatest wulver warriors in history. I've learned from t'best."

"But ye're not a wulver." Griff stated the obvious, in spite of the way she glowered at him. "And ye *are* a woman. Men, 'specially wulver men, have a physical advantage ye do'na. It's simple fact."

Griff gnawed on the leg of chicken, picking it cleanly of meat, before reaching for another, trying to ignore the holes the woman was trying to burn into him with her eyes. But she wasn't about it let it go.

Bridget's voice trembled just slightly as she leveled her gaze on him. "Ye're t'most arrogant... foolhardy..." Her eyes dropped to the chicken breast he held in his fingers. "Slob of a man I've *e'er* met."

Griff met her unwavering gaze. She was nearly smoldering, she was so angry. Out of the corner of his eye, he saw the older woman, Aleesa, frowning at her daughter's words.

"An' how many men've ye met?" Griff inquired politely, managing to keep most of the smirk off his face.

"What does't matter?" she asked, straightening her shoulders haughtily.

Griff shrugged one shoulder, reaching for his mug. "I need t'know yer frame'o'reference."

"He's insufferable!" Bridget exclaimed, looking across the table at her father. "I'm sorry I did'na best 'im fer ye. He does'na deserve whate'er knowledge he's 'ere t'seek. An' I do'na feel ye should give it t'him."

"How d'ye know anythin' about me?" Griff asked, still keeping his tone conversational. He wasn't going to take the girl's bait, no matter how she set the trap.

"I know enough." Bridget snapped a carrot between her teeth, chewing noisily. The vegetable clearly hadn't been fully cooked. "I know ye're full'o'pride. Ye're boastful, ye're rude, ye b'lieve ye're entitled. Not only t'whate'er 'tis ye wanna know 'bout t'lost packs'o'wulvers, but ye act as if ye're king of 'em a'ready."

"Bridget," Aleesa warned, shaking her head.

"Accordin' t'prophecy, I am." Griff smiled, a little smugly, he had to admit.

He heard Aleesa gasp, and she put her trembling mug back on the table to gape at him. Her blue eyes stared into his, her head cocked, and he knew she was seeing, maybe for the first time, the color of his eyes.

He wondered if they were their usual, strange, gold color, or if they had suddenly flared red. He sometimes could feel when it happened, especially when he was angry, but not always. The older man was watching too, a look on his face that had not been there previously. It wasn't frightened, like the dark-haired wulver woman, it was harder, more knowing, and resolute.

"Wha' prophecy?" Bridget looked between her parents, frowning, and then at Griff. "I know of no prophecy about t'king of wulvers. Ye're an arrogant, assumin' fool."

"Mayhaps ye do'na know as much as ye think ye do." Griff blinked at her and Bridget glared back, grinding her teeth. He could hear it.

"T'red wulver?" Aleesa's voice trembled almost as much as her mug had in its journey from hand to table. She glanced at her husband, meeting his eyes, and something passed between them.

The gray-haired wulver stood, towering at full height, looking down at Griff and snarling, "That's not a claim t'make lightly."

"It's mine t'make." Griff stood, too, and it happened so fast that both women at the table jumped back in shock when Griff shook his dark mane of hair and shifted instantly from man to wulver-warrior. His half-wolf form was formidable, twice his normal size, with a wolf's head but a man's body, his fur a dark russet color, his eyes blood red, flashing.

He didn't need to see himself to know.

He saw it in their eyes.

He saw it on Bridget's already pale face that went stark white at the sight of him.

Not to be outdone, the older man shifted, too. His mane of hair turned to gray fur and teeth, as the two wolf-men faced each other across the table, growling deep in their throats, threatening each other, dark lips pulled back from their canines in warning.

"Enough!" Aleesa cried, standing and holding a palm out to each wulver, as if she could keep them apart. "Violence's forbidden 'ere. If ye wanna 'ave a pissin' contest, go do it top side, d'ye hear me?"

Griff shifted back first, with a shake of his big, russet-colored wolf head, and the older man followed suit, but the tension hadn't eased in the slightest. Griff felt the hair still standing up on the back of his neck as he faced the gray-haired wulver.

"If he really *is* t'red wulver…" Aleesa murmured to her husband. The gray-haired man's lip curled, and Griff saw, he didn't know what to believe.

"I *am* t'red wulver," Griff insisted. He'd been called such in his own pack for so long, he wasn't used to being doubted. "Ye're addressin' yer future king."

"Ye're no one's king yet, pup." The other man leveled him with a long stare. "And ye're addressin' Alaric, t'Gray Ghost, swordmaster t'yer father, Raife, and 'is father a'fore 'im, and senior guardian of this temple. Ye'll stand down, or I'll be glad t'remind ye of yer place 'ere."

Griff had the impulse to fly across the table, to take him on here and now, but he saw the way Bridget glared at them, how Aleesa's eyes grew wide as she looked between the two men, and so he held back. They had information he wanted—needed. Mayhaps if he could convince them of the prophecy, and that he was the wulver who fulfilled it, they would be more forthcoming with that information.

"Alaric, t'Gray Ghost." Griff held his hand out to the other man, who took it, and they shook. "Yer reputation proceeds ye. M'father talked overmuch of yer swordsmanship and yer bravery. Now I know where t'lass learned it."

That broke the tension and they all sat down again to eat. He was surprised by the girl beside him, whose anger seemed to have ebbed away entirely. She just watched and listened as they talked around the table.

"So ye're really Raife's son?" Alaric asked, studying him. Both the wulvers looked at him quite differently now that they knew his parentage. That both pleased and annoyed him.

"Aye." Griff reached for the last leg of chicken at the same time as the woman beside him.

"Ye look like 'im." Aleesa nodded over her mug.

"More's the pity." Griff snorted, struggling with Bridget briefly over the leg of chicken. Another test of wills. He glanced at her, smiling, and she rolled her eyes and gave up, letting him have it.

"Except t'eyes," Alaric noted.

"How'd ye come t'be 'ere, in this temple?" Griff asked, leaning over and depositing the last chicken leg in his hand on Bridget's plate. "Story tells that yer wife went out t'gather herbs and ne'er returned?"

"Aye." Alaric nodded. "Aleesa had a dream 'bout this place. She was called 'ere, y'ken?"

"By... who?" Griff blinking, glancing around, as if another presence might suddenly appear and make themselves known, although he knew that was unlikely.

"I do'na know," Aleesa said softly, her gaze dropped to her plate. "T'was a voice from... far 'way, 'cross t'sea. I had t'follow."

"So ye left yer husband an' young pup?" Griff looked over at Bridget as she tossed the chicken leg back onto his plate.

"Pup?" Bridget asked, looking at her mother, clearly surprised.

"A daughter..." Aleesa did not lift her lowered eyes, and her voice dropped to something so soft it was hard to hear her. "Kirstin..."

"An' ye followed 'er?" Griff asked. He picked up the chicken leg, studying it. He no longer wanted it, would have let the girl have it, but she refused. That irked him.

"Aye," Alaric agreed, sliding a hand over his mate's on the table. "I followed, and I found 'er."

"How?" he asked. "How could ye know where she'd gone?"

"I did'na know," Alaric admitted, looking at his mate with the kind of love Griff was used to seeing pass between couples he knew—like his parents, like Laina and Darrow, Kirstin and Donal. He knew that kind of love when he saw it, even if it continued to baffle him. "I followed 'er trail at first. Then, later, I discovered a woman'd sought passage t'Skara Brae from t'place where her trail ended, and I knew't mus' be 'er. I challenged the guardian of this temple—an' I slew 'im."

"There was a guardian 'ere?" Griff stared at him in surprise as he quietly snuck the chicken leg onto Bridget's plate. The girl noticed and glanced at him, but she didn't say anything.

"Aye, but no priestess." Alaric patted his wife's hand. "Aleesa knew... t'was 'er callin'."

The dark-haired woman lifted her eyes to meet his and Griff saw tears there. It pained him. He knew the woman who was her daughter, who had been without her mother for years, who thought the woman was likely dead—and her father, as well.

"Ye know m'Kirstin?" Aleesa asked him softly. Her lower lip quivered. "She's well?"

"Aye," he replied, nodding. "Her son, Rory, is one of me truest friends."

"She has a son..." Aleesa looked over at her husband and something passed between them. How long had it been, Griff wondered, since the parents had seen their daughter? Forty years, mayhaps? The older wulver woman turned back to Griff, asking, "She found 'er one true mate, then?"

"Aye, The MacFalon." He had already told her he didn't believe in magic—he wasn't about to tell her he didn't believe in "one true mates" either.

"The... who?" Bridget looked blindsided. She'd forgotten the fought-over chicken leg. She'd probably even forgotten her loss to Griff at the crossroads, from the confused, surprised look on her face.

"Donal MacFalon," he explained. "Son of Lachlan. Brother of Alistair."

"My Kirstin's married t'The MacFalon?" Alaric's voice was as hard as granite.

"He's a fine man," Griff countered, shaking his head at the old man's alarm. He could understand it, of course. There was a time when The MacFalon—in fact, all of the MacFalon clan—had actively hunted and killed wulvers. But that wasn't the case anymore, not since the wolf pact. King Henry VII, who had an encounter with Griff's grandmother, from which his father, Raife, was born, had initiated the wolf pact. It had resulted in peaceable relations between the wulvers, Scots and English for years.

"He's a good husband an' father," Griff told them. "An' a trusted leader."

"He's still laird of the clan?" Aleesa asked, cocking her head in confusion.

"Aye. He was when I left." Griff chuckled. "They live in Castle MacFalon."

"How?" Aleesa frowned. "I know t'wolf pact was keepin' the peace b'tween 'em, but... I can'na imagine t'MacFalons allowin' wulvers t'live in t'castle."

"Heh. You'd be surprised." Griff grinned, remembering how often he was at Castle MacFalon, or Rory was visiting the den. They passed back and forth quite often with no incident. Just thinking about it made him a little homesick. "Besides, Kirstin's not a wulver anymore."

Alessa sat back, truly shocked, whispering, "What?"

"My mother, Sibyl—she's a human woman, not a wulver—she's a great healer," Griff explained. He tried to think of the best way to present things to her, but decided there wasn't really a good one. So he just told her. "She found a cure for t'wulver woman's curse. They found an old text buried in the first den, and she deciphered its meanin' enough to gather the herbs she needed to make a cure."

"The Book of the Moon Midwives?" Aleesa asked, her already wide eyes growing wider.

"Aye, how'd ye know?" Griff wondered aloud.

"I know of it," she breathed. Aleesa looked at her husband, then back at Griff, and finally, her gaze fell onto her daughter—the one who she had not borne, but raised. "No one knew where t'was. Tis where the prophecy's told."

"Aye, m'mother and the wulver women have been pouring over the thing for years." Griff snorted, sitting back in his chair. "M'mother could only read English. But she got help from Moira and Beitrus."

"Beitrus..." A smile flitted across Aleesa's face. "She's still alive, then?"

"Aye, old as t'hills, startin' t'go blind." Griff smiled back at her. "...and she's no longer a wulver either."

"What?" Aleesa exclaimed.

"She's the one who tested t'cure," Griff told her. "Insisted, as she was t'oldest, and had t'least t'lose, if it killed 'er."

"They let 'er just take it?" Alaric cried.

Griff chuckled. "No, but if ye knew Beitrus—she's stubborn."

"Aye, that she is." Aleesa laughed, patting her husband's hand. "Always was."

"Why'd ye never send word?" Griff asked, looking between the two older wulvers with a slow shake of his head. "At least tell us ye were 'ere?"

"I can'na leave." Tears sprang to Aleesa's eyes again and she blinked them quickly away when her daughter looked at her. "Once a priestess commits 'erself to this temple, she can'na go."

"Yer daughter would've liked to know ye were alive," Griff said softly. He saw his words hurt her, but he felt they had to be said. "Safe."

"All is as it should be." Alaric stood, leaning over to kiss the top of his wife's bent head.

"Yer 'ere now." Aleesa lifted her gaze to meet Griff's, such hope in her eyes. "Ye can carry word back to m'Kirstin, can't ye?"

Griff nodded. "Aye."

The woman stood, too, helping her husband and daughter clear the table. Griff moved to help them, but Aleesa insisted, as their guest, that he sit.

"The Book of the Moon Midwives." Aleesa shook her head in disbelief as she made them all more tea. "I'd like t'see it. Read it—what I could make out. Ye could read it t'me, Alaric."

Bridget sat beside him, holding her own cup of tea. She was quiet now, far more subdued. Clearly he had brought new and mayhaps not welcome information into this little, isolated family. He worried about the way her brow wrinkled as she blew gently on the hot liquid, looking into it as if it might hold some answers.

"All t'wulvers in m'den can read'n'write both Gaelic'n'English," Griff told Aleesa. "M'mother was English—but she learned Gaelic right alongside t'pups."

"They read'n'write?" Alaric's eyes widened.

"Aye. She's big on education." Griff laughed. "And had quite an influence over m'father."

"I guess so." Alaric laughed too, shaking his head.

"I don't see much point in knowin' how t'read'n'write." Griff shrugged. "If wulvers were meant t'be men, we wouldn't be half-wolf, eh?"

"So you've seen t'prophecy written?" Aleesa asked, looking at him in wonder.

"No, I've heard it told," Griff replied. He'd heard so much about it, his whole life, he really didn't care to actually read the words. "M'mother, m'aunts, all t'healers've poured over that book backwards'n'forwards, since t'day I was born."

"What's this prophecy?" Bridget spoke up, frowning between Griff and her parents.

"I thought, mayhaps, t'was just legend," Aleesa told her daughter. "But if they've found t'book... if The Book of the Moon Midwives exists..."

"Oh, aye, it exists," Griff assured her. "That's how I found out 'bout t'lost packs."

"There's a prophecy 'bout a red wulver who'll bring together t'lost packs," Aleesa explained to her daughter. "I did'na know it would e'er come to pass in m'lifetime…"

Bridget sighed, looking at Griff, narrowing her gaze at him. "Yer this red wulver?"

"So they say." He shrugged. If it served him to be the red wulver here, in this temple, then he would be that red wulver. If it got him what he wanted—the location of the lost, leaderless packs—then so be it.

"If he's t'red wulver this prophecy speaks of…" Bridget put her mug on the table, leaning in to look at the other priestess. "Mother, only t'dragon can tell us fer sure."

"Dragon?" Griff's hand went to his empty sheath. He hated being unarmed. It was like walking around naked.

"Come." Aleesa nodded, holding a hand out to Griff.

"Where're we goin'?" he asked as they all rose. He didn't like the sound of this.

"To t'sacred pool," Bridget told him, a small smile playing on her lips. "Mayhaps t'find t'very thing ye seek."

⚬

Griff hesitated at the edge of the so-called sacred pool, watching Alaric take up as guardian across from him, arms folded. The men stood, simply a witness as the women busied themselves with bowls of herbs and ceremonial swords.

He had sought this place out in hopes of finding information about the lost packs, but now that he was here, he wasn't quite so sure that he wanted to know, after all. He'd dismissed the idea of the prophecy his whole life. In part, because his mother had been doubtful of it herself. She didn't come from the wulver world, even if she now lived in it, and she'd never quite believed that it was her son's destiny to fulfill some wulver prophecy.

Mayhaps that was only because she had wished it wasn't so, he thought, watching as the two women faced each other across the pool, chanting softly. The light in the sky overhead had changed, and the slant that came in from above hinted that it was past supper time. They had talked long at the table as they feasted, he realized now.

Aleesa had been overcurious about her daughter, not that he could blame her. But he had little understanding of the woman. How could she leave her husband and infant daughter and set out for this place, when she hadn't even known it existed?

Aleesa said she had been called here to the Temple of Ardis and Asher. By what? By whom? Griff glanced around, his senses keen, sniffing the air, getting the scent of herbs, the heather and the silvermoon, a heady combination. He felt no other presence here, heard no voices. The dark-haired woman didn't seem consumed by madness or melancholy, aside from a natural longing in missing her offspring.

Mayhaps a temporary madness, then, when she made her way here to Skara Brae?

But what had kept her? He wondered. After Alaric found his wife, why had he not brought her home? They had a small child they'd both abandoned back at their den, and for what? To guard an empty temple, to chant over some quiet pool? Ridiculous.

It saddened him, watching the two women as they stood, facing each other, ceremonial swords held aloft. So many years wasted, the two of them alone—and now this young woman they were training to take their place. He watched her, the way her auburn hair brushed her cheek as she bent her head, how her eyelashes trembled when she closed them over those bright green eyes, and felt a longing he didn't quite understand.

Mayhaps it was just that the girl was trying very hard to live up to someone else's image of her. That much was clear—and he could definitely relate.

That's when the swords caught flame.

Griff reached for his own sword, then realized, again, that it was no longer at his side. Across the pool, Alaric stood watching, unalarmed. Another trick then? The light overhead, cast in a certain way? Griff cocked his head, this way and that, frowning as the women chanted, louder and louder, in a language that sounded familiar, and yet he couldn't quite make out full words. Then they began to repeat one word in Gaelic, over and over, one he did know—dragon.

Arach. Arach. Arach.

Something changed in the room. A shift, movement, mayhaps just the flutter of a breeze, but Griff felt it tickle his skin, like a coming storm. Something was rising. It hung there, like impending doom, expectant, waiting. He found himself holding his breath, his senses heightened. The hair stood up on his arms and the back of his neck. The red-haired woman, Bridget, stared into the pool, her sword still appearing to glow, but the fire had gone from a normal orange to something blueish silver.

Griff's gaze followed hers and, deep in the pool, he saw a face. Leaning closer, for a moment, he thought it was just his own reflection—*it must be*—but then it began to rise, higher and higher, as if it was diving up from the depths. His heart thumped hard in his ears, the way it always did before a good battle was about to begin, and again, his hand went for his sword, finding only an empty scabbard.

Then, the dragon appeared.

It was there—and not there. A dragon's head, all long neck and wide, flaring nostrils, its eyes looking straight at Griff. He saw the image of the dragon, and yet, he saw through it, too, could look right into and past it to see Alaric standing on the opposite side of the pool, Aleesa to his left, Bridget to his right. They were all there, staring at the image of the dragon, transfixed.

Griff shook his head, doing everything in his power to keep from going full-on wolf and attacking the image in front of him. He knew it wasn't real—*couldn't* be real. He would simply embarrass himself and jump straight into the water, and then have to drag himself out and shake off like a wet dog.

Griff held himself back, staring at the dragon, who stared right back at him.

He felt it happening, before he heard them gasp. His eyes were turning red, mirroring the dragon's own blood-red gaze. Usually, when his eyes turned, he was feeling something very strong—mostly anger. Although, to his chagrin, his mother used to like to tell people that every time she nursed him, his eyes would turn red. But now, in this moment, he wasn't feeling anger—an emotion he often associated with strength.

No, he was on edge, certainly, senses more alive than they might ever have been in his entire life, at least while he was in human form, but it wasn't anger that filled him now.

It was power.

Pure, raw, unadulterated power.

He felt as if he, like the image of the dragon before him, could simply spread wings and fly away. He could burn cities to the ground with a simple sneeze. Fry a man to a crisp with a cough. And if he wanted to? He could rule them all.

Griff struggled to contain this feeling, to make sense of it. Gory hell, even his cock was hard with excitement—he felt like he had another sword under his plaid!

Then the dragon turned its head. It had no body Griff could see—mayhaps the rest of it was buried in the pool. He knew this thought would drive him mad if he lingered on it, trying to find the rest of the dragon who couldn't really exist that appeared before him and filled him with such feeling.

But then the beast turned its scaly head and looked at Bridget.

Griff moved without thinking. He saw it happen—saw the beast's eyes flash silver, instead of red, saw Bridget's eyes, like an answering call, flash silver, too. That grey-green moved all the way to the other end of the spectrum, her eyes glowing, like someone gone blind.

"No!" Griff charged, leaping over the corner of the pool to cut the distance, nearly losing his footing on the slippery rock as he tackled the young woman, her ceremonial sword still flaming, aloft, pointing at the dragon's head rising up from the center of the water.

He heard the other woman, Aleesa, cry out, heard Alaric shout, but he paid neither of them any mind as he covered Bridget's body with his own, taking her down to the wet rocks with him.

Bridget's sword dropped, hissing into the water behind them. She cried out as he covered her, mindful of his weight, not to crush her, just to keep her safe from harm. She stared up at him in wonder, their eyes locked, and for a moment he saw himself, the red heat of his own eyes reflected in the silver pools of hers.

"Griff," she whispered, and he felt the way his cock hardened at the sound of his name in her mouth. His erection strained against the soft, silky material of her robe, and beyond that, against her incredible softness. He had never wanted a woman more than he wanted her in that moment, and if Alaric hadn't called his name, too, he might have rolled her over and taken her without thinking—right then, right there.

"Are y'all right, lass?" Griff asked, his voice hoarse with emotion.

"I did'na need rescuing!" Bridget struggled under him, movements that didn't make him any less hard for her. In fact, quite the opposite. She pushed against his chest with both hands—the woman had a surprising amount of strength for a human girl, even without armor and a sword. "Ye're such an impetuous fool! The dragon'n't'lady could've told ye what ye wanted t'know."

"What?" Griff puzzled at her words. "What lady?"

"Did ye n'see 'er?" She wiggled out from under him and he saw that her robe was in disarray, parting slightly in the front, giving him a view of her pale, creamy thigh. Griff saw her noticing him looking at the gap in her robe and she pulled it closed, color rising to her cheeks. "If ye had'na interrupted, ye would've seen 'er. She was turning t'me. Did ye n'see 'er eyes go silver?"

"I only saw... t'dragon..." He frowned, moving to his feet, feeling a little lightheaded in the aftermath. He held a hand out to help her up and she made a face, ignoring it once again and standing on her own.

"Father?" Bridget frowned, glancing behind Griff, and he turned to see both Alaric and Aleesa approaching. The look on both their faces startled him, but what they did next left him truly speechless for the first time in his whole life.

"What're ye doin'?" Bridget blinked as both of her parents took a knee before Griff, bowing their heads.

"Y'are t'one true king," Alaric said, a slight quiver in his voice, gray head bowed. "How can we serve ye?"

What in the gory hell was he supposed to say to that? Griff stared at them, alarmed. Then he looked at Bridget. It was the fear in her eyes that forced words from his throat. He took the matter in hand as best he could.

"Firs' of all, ye can get up." Griff huffed, rolling his eyes. He gave them both a hand up, which they accepted, unlike their daughter, who still stood, tall and haughty and disbelieving, beside him. "And then ye can tell me where t'find t'lost packs. Tis all I wanna know."

"Alas, we can'na tell ye." Aleesa looked distraught, wringing her hands, looking at Alaric. "We do'na know."

"But we can show ye where tis written," Alaric replied.

"A'righ'," Griff sighed with impatience. "I s'pose that's t'next best thing."

"Except..." Aleesa bit her lip.

"What?" Griff threw up his hands. "T'book's hidden? We have t'tunnel t'the center of the country mayhaps?"

"No, it has t'be high moon time," Alaric informed him. "That'll be jus' a few days from now."

"Aye, a'course." Griff ran a hand through his hair, wondering how in the world he was going to wait, even a few days in this place—for a full moon, of all things. "Do t'stars hafta be in alignment, too? Mayhaps I have t'strip naked an 'dance 'round a fire while ye chant?"

"Aye, tis exactly righ'." Bridget looked at him, unblinking, a little smile playing on her lips. "Ye hafta dance naked 'round a fire under t'full moon."

"Bridget, hush." Her mother sighed. "T'dragon will'na return now. We'll hafta wait for t'high moon."

"If I hafta wait..." Griff sighed, too. He hated waiting. "Can I trouble ye fer a bed, mayhaps?"

"A'course." Aleesa nodded. "I'll make up a bed fer ye."

"And, while I'm thinking on it... a bath?" he suggested hopefully. He hadn't bathed since the day of the Great Hunt, and the pool in front of him looked very inviting.

"Aye." Aleesa smiled at him, putting a soft hand on his forearm. "I'll start boilin' water, m'lord."

"M'lord?" Bridget snorted under her breath and Griff glanced at her, remembering the way she felt underneath him, all softness pressed between the stone and the rigid resistance of his body.

"Pardon?" He cocked an eyebrow at her.

"Who d'ye think y're, a king?" Bridget exclaimed, crossing her arms and glaring at him.

"Aye." He chuckled, glancing at Aleesa and seeing her frown. Clearly the wulvers were now on his side, even if the girl was not. He told Aleesa, "And I'd like 'er to tend me."

"I will not—" Bridget protested, her eyes widening.

"Aye, lass, ye will!" Aleesa's eyes flashed, not silver or red, but there were some things far worse than curses and prophecies, and clearly Aleesa's temper was one of them. Griff grinned as Aleesa took her daughter's arm, yanking her out of the room. "Now come wit' me."

Chapter Four

Bridget grumbled to herself the entire time as she carried buckets of hot water back and forth from the fire to fill the wooden tub. She had it halfway full, and the floor was wet where she'd splashed—not to mention the front of her robe, which clung to her like a damned second skin—when the big wulver-man, Griff, came into the room. He glanced at her as she put the last two full buckets on the floor beside the fireplace in his room. These were for rinsing, of course.

"Are ye ready fer yer bath, m'lord?" She couldn't keep the venom from dripping off her tongue.

First, this beast bests her as temple guardian. Then, he somehow bewitches her parents into thinking he's some sort of "red wulver" who's here to fulfill a prophecy. Then, just when the dragon and the lady were about to tell them the truth, he attacks her!

Rescue, my foot, she thought, glaring as the man began to undress. His sheath was empty—no swords, aside from the ceremonial ones, were allowed in the temple—and he tossed it onto the bed.

Alaric and Aleesa had given up their room, with the big bed and large fireplace, for their guest. And why? Because they thought this arrogant fool was some sort of wulver king? He was nothing but a bragging, boastful boy.

Bridget turned to watch him, leaning against the tub, arms crossed over her chest. Well, mayhaps not so much a boy, she corrected herself, as he pulled his tunic over his head, tossing it on the bed, too. At least, not physically. His shoulders were big and broad, tawny colored in the firelight. He was so muscled, the hills and valleys in his arms alone were breathtaking, like the scenery of Skara Brae. Rolling and rather delicious.

Bridget told herself it was the heat from the fire, and her own toil in carrying water back and forth from the kitchen, that made her face flush when the man divested himself of his plaid. He half-sat on the bed, pulling off hose and boots too, tossing them aside.

She knew Aleesa would want them washed, and so Bridget moved to retrieve them. She set them all by the door—his clothes, boots, sword sheath, belt—ignoring the fact that he was naked behind her.

She averted her eyes when he climbed into the tub, but she couldn't help seeing the bulge of the man's strong thighs, the hollows at the sides of his buttocks, before he sank into the water with a low, soft groan.

"What d'ye wan' me t'do?" Bridget had hissed at her mother as they warmed water over the fire.

"Jus' tend 'im, Bridget," Aleesa told her with a heavy sigh. "Wash t'man wit' soap'n'water. Ye act like ye do'na know what a bath is!"

Of course she knew what a bath was. She'd taken thousands. Okay, maybe hundreds. But she'd never had to wash anyone but herself before. She didn't know anything about man parts, aside from the fact that, if you brought a knee up between their legs, they had soft stones that puckered and shriveled and turned them into howling babies. She'd learned that lesson by accident, but her father had used it, as he used everything, to teach her a lesson. If she absolutely had to hurt a man, if he was besting her and she had to escape, honorably or no, that was the best way to do so.

"Ye can leave me, lass," Griff called softly as Bridget put his things in order. Mayhaps she was stalling, it was true. "I can bathe m'self."

She glanced over, seeing his head tipped back, eyes closed, his big arms resting on the sides of the tub, elbows cocked, hands floating in the water. When she didn't answer, he peeped one eye open to look at her. She stood near the door, undecided, worrying her lip between her teeth. Griff opened two eyes, then his gaze moved down her robe, all the way to her bare toes peeking out from underneath, then upwards until their eyes locked.

"D'ye 'ave any soap, lass?" he asked, running a hand through his thick, dark mass of hair. It curled even more when it was wet, she noticed.

"Aye," she said softly, moving to get it for him. She had made the soap herself. Aleesa taught her that, the same way she'd taught her how to chant and throw herbs into the scrying pool. Her own soap smelled of heather and silvermoon, but this was sage and cedar, a far more masculine scent they made for Alaric, who protested going around smelling like flowers—when they could get him to bathe, that was.

Griff lifted it to his nose, sniffing it lightly, giving her an appreciative look as he soaped up his hands and began rubbing them over his chest. She noticed the hairs that curled there, circling his nipples, small and pink, like miniatures of her own. Hers were hard—probably because she'd gotten herself soaked carrying all the water back and forth, she told herself, trying to ignore the soft pulse between her thighs.

He had told her to go, but she didn't. Instead, she knelt by the side of the tub, her eyes glued to the way his hands roamed his chest and shoulders and arms, wondering what it felt like to map that fleshy terrain. His hands dipped under the water with the soap, toward areas she didn't dare peek at.

Her mother had bid her to tend the man, and so Bridget reached for a washing cloth, dipping it into the water to wet it, and then holding her hand out to him silently for the soap.

Griff looked at her for a moment, a bemused smile playing on his lips, but he handed it over, watching as she rubbed soap into the cloth, making suds.

"How'd ye come t'be 'ere, Bridget?" Griff asked, leaning forward when she put a hand on his shoulder and pulled.

"Tis m'home," she said simply, standing and moving in behind him so she could scrub his back. His flesh was beautifully tanned, his shoulder blades jutting like wings as he let her scrub, up and down, back and forth. He gave a little groan when she rubbed the cloth hard over his shoulders.

"Ye like that?" She cocked her head, her fingers digging into the muscle, and he gave another soft moan.

"Aye." He rolled his head from side to side. "T'was a long journey."

"Where d'ye come from?" she asked, wondering about it, knowing now that his pack had been the same that her parents had left. They had once lived in the same den. "Where's yer home?"

"Scotland," he told her, glancing back in surprise at her question. He was wondering why her parents hadn't told her. And she was wondering the same thing. "Middle March. Right on t'border b'tween Scotland'n'England. We used t'have a mountain den, back a'fore I was born. M'mother says t'was lovely, wit' a valley contained in t'mountain range, an' a stream runnin' through it. Now we live in a den underground—on MacFalon land. Tis a beautiful place. Reminds me of this."

"I've ne'er known any other home but this," she admitted, her fingers digging into the hard, bunched muscle of his shoulders. He let out a sigh of relief at her touch, and another groan when she dug her thumbs into his flesh. "I'm not hurtin' ye?"

"No, lass." He chuckled. "Not likely."

She stiffened at his words, withdrawing, knowing he was referring to their first meeting.

"Do'na stop." He looked back at her in the firelight. "I did'na mean t'insult ye. It's jus'… I've ne'er met a woman like ye a'fore."

"What's that mean?" She frowned, but she put her hands back onto his shoulders, continuing to knead his flesh like bread dough. He moaned again, eyes closing. He really seemed to like it, and for some reason, that pleased her. "Griff?"

"Hmmm?" His head tilted forward as she dug her fingers into his shoulder blades.

"What d'ye mean, ye've ne'er met a woman like me?"

"Where I come from," he said, hissing when she scraped him lightly with her nails. "Women do'na fight. Wulver women… they're not warriors."

"Ye do'na think a woman should be a warrior?" She frowned, watched the water trickling down his skin in little rivers. There were no scars or marks on the man, and she wondered at it, but then she remembered—he was a wulver. A warrior, like Alaric.

She had once nicked her trainer with her long sword, a gash in his arm that would have taken her months to heal from—and would have left a very bad scar—but on Alaric, the wound had closed up in moments. Within a quarter of an hour, there was no sign it had even happened at all.

"Yer a fine swordma—swords*woman*." He corrected himself, smiling back at her. "He's trained ye vera well. Ye gave me quite a beatin' out there, lass. I was afeared I was'na gonna make't into t'temple after all."

"Now you're just humorin' me…" She rolled her eyes, poking him in the shoulder with her finger.

"Mayhaps a lil." His smile spread into a mischievous grin. "But tell me t'truth… d'ye wanna be a warrior?"

"What d'ye mean?" She wrinkled her nose at him, cocking her head. "I've been trained t'be t'temple guardian'n'priestess. Tis what I'm meant t'do."

"Hm." Griff's gaze moved to the fire. In this light, his eyes were almost gold. "Mayhaps."

"Ye came 'ere because of a prophecy," she reminded him. "Ye mus' b'lieve in destiny."

"Ye'd think so." He snorted. "Y'know, the Scots—they let women lead their clans. The MacFalon's trained 'is daughters right alongside 'is sons."

"The MacFalon..." Bridget frowned, remembering their conversation at dinner. It seemed a million years ago now, but the things that had been revealed at that meal had changed everything for her. She couldn't look at her parents now without feeling a sense of loss and betrayal. Why had they not told her where they'd come from, what they'd left behind?

"M'father's told me stories about the Scots—and The MacFalon," she told him. It was true, but only in a general sense. Alaric had told her about a pact between wulvers and men that had been drafted by the king of England himself.

"Different man, I promise ye." Griff assured her, seeing her expression as she moved the washing cloth over his shoulder, down his arm, as she came to kneel beside the tub. "Donal MacFalon would'na hurt a wulver. He married one."

"Kirstin..." It was the first time Bridget had said the girl's name aloud, and it pained her greatly. Her parents, the people who had loved and raised her from infancy, had another daughter. And she had never known. How could it be?

Griff's wet hand touched her face, tilting her chin up so she was forced to meet his eyes. She knew he would see the tears there, the ones she'd been trying to hide. Her breath caught, her throat closing up, and she felt her lip tremble as he searched her face with those strange-colored eyes of his.

"Ye did'na know they had a child, did ye?" he asked softly.

"No." She barely whispered the word. One of the tears that threatened trembled on her lashes and fell down her cheek.

"Yer not their own." He wiped her cheek with his wet thumb, frowning. The look on his face made her want to sob—everything she was feeling was reflected in his eyes. Her anger, her sadness, bewilderment, confusion.

"They took me in," she told him, reminding herself of this fact. They were the only parents she'd ever known, and they loved her. She knew that was true.

"How old were ye?" He leaned back as she soaped the cloth again, washing his shoulders, his collarbone. He seemed to like it when she rubbed hard, so she did so.

"Jus' a bairn," she said, making him lift his arms so she could scrub underneath. "M'mother says someone left me at t'temple, near t'secret entrance."

"The one in t'rock?"

"Aye." She traced the cloth down the center of his chest, between his ribs.

"How'd they know t'was there?"

"I do'na know." She shrugged, grazing the cloth over the row of hills and valleys that made up the man's abdomen. It was hard as rock, so unlike her own softness. "M'father thinks t'was a mage who knew there were guardians at t' temple who'd care fer me—and train me t'be like them."

"Tis strange, leavin' a human child wit' two wulvers." Griff watched her move the washing cloth lower. His eyes were darker now, almost orange. "How'd they know you'd not be breakfast?"

"But they did'na eat me." She laughed. The man had a line of dark hair that ran from his navel down under the water and she traced that with the cloth, too, fascinated. "All is as it should be."

"Ye keep sayin' that." Griff tilted his head at her.

"Tis true." She shrugged, wetting her lips—her mouth felt suddenly dry—when she saw the appendage between his legs had grown in size, pointing directly at her. She knew enough about mating—animals, humans and wulvers—to know what it meant. But Bridget found herself fascinated by it. She wanted nothing more than to reach down and touch him.

"If ye do what yer thinkin' of, lass, ye'll n'leave this room a maiden," he told her, voice low, and she startled, blinking up at him in surprise. "Not that I'll stop ye..."

"Oh... I..." She cleared her throat, leaning back, gripping the edge of the tub, and saw the way his gaze dropped to her breasts. Her nipples were achingly hard and completely visible through the thin, wet material of her white robe. She glanced down at them, and saw they were like little pink pebbles. Ripe cherries, waiting to be plucked and devoured.

"Ye've ne'er been with a man," he remarked. His voice was low, matter-of-fact, and it moved over her like a caress.

"I'm t'be a temple priestess," she confessed, swallowing past some sort of obstruction in her throat. "As well as a guardian."

"So ye mus' retain yer maidenhood, then, aye?" Griff inquired, eyebrows going up just slightly, waiting for her response.

"I… no…" She shook her head, denying it, although why she was so quick to do so, she didn't understand. Just like she didn't understand her body's response to this man's closeness—and his nudity. "A priestess mus' be whole in herself. Aleesa is no maiden, nor was she when she came 'ere. But a priestess mus'na be subservient to anyone—man or woman."

"Aleesa isn't subservient to Alaric then?" Griff asked. "But they're mates, aren't they?'

"Aye," she agreed, frowning. "But their marriage is that of equals. Aleesa holds far more power here than Alaric."

"I do'na understand." The man puzzled this out, brow drawn. "A man is naturally more powerful than a woman."

"Physically mayhaps." A smile played on Bridget's lips at his assumptions. "But energetically, a woman'll always be more powerful than a man. She's t'ocean, t'weather, t'very air ye breathe. She's t'life giver. N'man can say that."

"Has any man e'er told ye how beautiful ye're, Bridget?" He reached a hand out to rub a thumb over the line of her jaw. He stopped at her chin, his thumb moving over her bottom lip, back and forth. He seemed fascinated with her mouth and she swallowed, trying to take in the man's words. Earlier, he had infuriated her with his arrogance and sense of entitlement. He had come here assuming he would best the temple guardian, gain entrance to their sacred space, and then find and exploit whatever information he could glean from them. She didn't feel him deserving of the knowledge contained here, even if he had bested her.

But in the end, that was her own failing—if Alaric had been the one to confront him, mayhaps things would have been different?

But now, here in this room, with the two of them alone, he didn't strike her as overconfident. He'd let his guard down, and she wondered at it. His words didn't matter to her—although when he told her she was beautiful, something ignited inside of her she didn't quite recognize or comprehend—as much as the soft look in his eyes when he told her.

"M'father's told me I'm beautiful." Bridget cleared her throat, using the soap in her hands to create suds. "Now close yer eyes, wulver. I'm gonna wash yer hair."

"Aye, mistress." Griff dutifully closed his eyes as she stood to run her hands through his hair. It was thick, even wet, and she used her fingernails to scrape his scalp, hearing him give a little growling noise in his throat in response. "So tell me, Bridget, d'ye really believe e'erythin' happens as it should?"

"Aye," she agreed, moving around the tub to retrieve a bucket of warm water to rinse him. "Tis all as it should be."

"How can ye say that?" Griff wondered, opening his eyes as she approached with the bucket—but his gaze was on her body in her robe, the way it clung to her skin. "I mean... yer parents abandoned ye..."

"Mayhaps." She lifted the bucket, looking pointedly at him. "Close yer eyes, wulver."

He did, reluctantly, and she poured the bucket over his head, washing the suds away. She took a bit too much pleasure in the way he sputtered and rubbed his face with his hands at the onslaught of water.

"Mayhaps they no longer live," Bridget mused. "Mayhaps they could'na care fer me. I do'na know. But Alaric'n'Aleesa've been t'best family I could've asked fer."

"But livin' here?" Griff rubbed his eyes with his thumbs and focused on her, frowning. "Ne'er leavin'?"

"Oh, I can leave," she told him, smiling. "Before I take m'vows as priestess, I can come'n'go as I please. I go hunting. I trap small game. I fish. I jus' do'na wander too far from t'temple."

"But they cannot leave?" Griff pondered this, glancing at the closed bedroom door.

"Aleesa can'na." She shook her head. "I do'na know what'd happen if she tried. And Alaric—he will ne'er leave her. The Temple of Ardis'n'Asher was meant always t'have both a guardian an' a priestess. They complement one another. Male an' female. Masculine an' feminine. He protects an' contains, and that allows 'er life force t'flow. He's t'riverbank, and she's t'water, ye ken?"

"Tis madness," Griff murmured, frowning as she leaned her hands against the side of the tub. She realized, then, that he was looking at her body in her robe, and her breasts were eye-level to him.

"Tis love," she countered softly. "An' devotion."

"I do'na understand. Help me understand," he lifted his gaze to hers, real confusion on his face. "How could she jus' leave?"

"Did ye n'leave?" Bridget asked, arching an eyebrow at him, seeing him startle a little. A flash of guilt crept into his eyes and she wondered who he was thinking about back home. Who had this man, this wulver, left behind? A mate? A child? The thought made her throat want to close up for some reason and she cleared it, standing and crossing her arms over her breasts to cover herself.

"Aye, I left," he admitted, running a hand through his dark, wet hair. "But I left no one behind."

"No one?" Bridget swallowed, waiting for his answer. She didn't know why it suddenly mattered to her so much, but it did.

"M'mother…" He shrugged a shoulder, and there was that flash of guilt again. Then his face hardened. "M'father."

She nodded, pursing her lips, eyes narrowed at him. "No one else?"

"Friends, kin…" He shrugged again, then a smile began at the corners of his mouth. "Why? What're ye askin', lass? Certainly no pups."

No pups. Something in her chest loosened. That must mean, then…

"No mate?" She just asked him directly, giving up on trying to hide what she wanted to know.

"No, lass." That bright, knowing look in his eyes made her want to smack him—or kiss him. She wasn't sure which.

"So," she mused. "You haven't found your true—"

"I do'na b'lieve in true mates," Griff growled, holding up his palm in protest, as if he could hold back the phrase "one true mate" from even being uttered. "I do'na b'lieve in magic. An' I do'na b'lieve in prophecies."

Bridget couldn't help smiling at this. "What *do* ye b'lieve in?"

"M'self." He crossed his arms over his chest, mirroring her.

"Why'm I n'surprised?" She laughed, and then did so again, even harder, when he scowled at her.

"What d'*ye* b'lieve in, then?"

"Magic." She said this first, not that it wasn't true. It was. But she also liked the way this fact seemed to irk him. "The divine. Love."

"Tomfoolery." He rolled his eyes, dismissing it all with the wave of his hand. "Nonsense."

"Ye came 'ere 'cause of a prophecy, wulver," she reminded him, delighting in the way his jaw hardened and his eyes flashed. They weren't red, like they had been when they mirrored the dragon's in the pool, but they were close.

"I came 'ere t'find m'kin," he said through lips that barely moved.

"Aye, an' ye succeeded." She nodded toward the door, meaning Aleesa and Alaric.

"I came 'ere t'find'n'reunite t'lost packs," he replied with a shake of his head. "If there're more wulvers in t'world, I wanna find 'em."

"Is that n'yer destiny?" she asked softly, remembering what her mother had said at dinner. "Is that n'what t'prophecy says t'red wulver'll do? Reunite t'lost packs?"

"I do'na care a rat's ass 'bout t'prophecy!" Griff's eyes were definitely red now. She stared at them, fascinated. It was as if a fire had been lit inside of him. Did he know, she wondered, when his eyes did that? "I wanna lead a pack of wulvers. If I was born t'do anythin', I was born t'do that."

"Tis all as it should be, then." She smiled at the way that stopped him—at least for the moment.

"Stop sayin' that," he finally snapped, asking, "D'ye 'ave any wine in this place?"

"Aye." She nodded, doing her best to hide the smile that irked him so much, making her way over to the table near the fireplace. Her mother had left a bottle of their best wine, thinking the wulver might want to indulge. She'd tasted the stuff, but only ceremonially.

She poured a glass, bringing it to him.

"Why d'ye n'wanna hear 'bout yer destiny?" she asked, handing him the mug. He drank from it, meeting her questioning gaze over the rim.

"'Cause tis jus' magical nonsense," he protested, then he looked at the cup. "This is good."

"More?" She glanced into the cup and brought the bottle back over, filling it again. "I'd think ye'd like knowin' yer destiny. That ye had a place in t'world."

"I'm bigger than m'destiny," Griff said simply, a statement that served to stop her. Bridget's breath caught as she looked at him, incredulous. Was he so arrogant, then, so full of himself?

"Ye think so?" She blinked at him.

"I know so." He glowered at the fire, that red color back in his eyes as he drank his wine.

Bridget went over and poured herself a glass of wine, taking a sip. He was right, it was good. It burned her throat a little and made her eyes water, but it was good. He glanced at her as she took a seat beside him on the stool they used to get in and out of the tub. The fire was warm and the wine made her feel even warmer.

"S'ye wanna be a leader," she mused, sipping her wine. "Like yer father?"

"Aye." His frown deepened. "M'father's a great leader. But I wanna lead m'own pack."

"What if t'lost packs a'ready 'ave a leader?" she asked, thinking aloud.

"Then they would'na be lost would they?" He sighed. "Can y'imagine what tis like t'be lost? Leaderless? T'have no pack?"

"Aye." She nodded, feeling the weight of his words. Alaric and Aleesa were her family, had always been, since she could remember. But this man, this wulver, reminded her quite painfully that they were not really her family. She didn't belong with them, to them. They weren't even her same kind.

They had a family. Another daughter.

Bridget finished her wine and poured herself more from the bottle.

"Aye, I s'pose, ye can."

She felt his wet fingertips brush her cheek, moving hair away from her face, and she glanced at him. His eyes weren't red anymore. They were back to that strange gold color, and his expression was thoughtful.

"I wanna bring t'lost packs home. We're a'ready outgrowin' our den. Mayhaps, when I return wit' t'lost packs, we can move back t'the mountain den. Tis bigger, more accommodatin', and there, mayhaps, I can lead our pack."

"But yer father... Raife?" She looked at him, questioning, and he nodded. "Is he n'the leader?"

"Aye, he is now." Griff gave a little nod. "But when I return home wit' t'lost packs, he'll know I'm ready t'lead. T'will be m'time."

For some reason, Bridget was thinking about taking her vows. It would be soon. And then... then she would be finally fulfilling her destiny. It was something she'd always believed, had always known. She'd grown up her whole life knowing it, understanding it, not even questioning it.

So why was she questioning it now?

"I hope ye find 'em," she said, putting a hand on his arm. Water beaded his skin, making it slippery to the touch. "I really hoped t'dragon an' the lady would help ye, but now..."

"Ye saw that, too?" Griff's voice dropped, shaking his head. The wine was loosening his tongue, she thought. Breaking down those barriers he had put up against things that couldn't be explained. Like magic. Like love. "I thought mayhaps I was dreamin'... or seein' things."

"Ye were seein' things," she said softly, finishing her wine. "Ye saw t'dragon."

"I saw *somethin'*," he admitted, holding his cup out, and she obliged, filling it. "I thought... I thought ye were in danger."

"Far less danger than when I faced ye at the crossroads," she teased, smiling when he looked at her. His gaze moved over her again, his eyes gone from gold to a rich, dark amber. His gaze moved to the V her robe made above her breasts and he frowned, reaching out to press a finger below her collarbone.

"Did I do this?" Griff touched the purple discoloration of the bruise there. Bridget saw it when she glanced down.

"Mayhaps." Bridget shrugged, setting her cup aside. The wine was making her head fuzzy. She was remembering the way he had pinned her against the rock, how thick and hard his thigh had been between her own. "I do'na remember. Tis nothin'."

"If there was such a thing as magic, I'd make it disappear." Griff stroked her bruise, frowning at it, as if it displeased him. It was an intimate gesture. Bridget felt very warm all of a sudden.

"There *is* magic, Griff."

He looked up when she said his name, his gaze moving slowly from her eyes to her mouth. She could almost feel his thumb there, the way he'd rubbed her lips. That made her feel even warmer.

"Can ye prove it?" A smile played on his lips.

"Magic's jus' nature doin' what it does naturally."

"So *e'erything* is magic?" he scoffed. His thumb moved over her collarbone, lightly stroking. Her nipples were so hard they hurt. He was looking at them, and that just made them ache even more.

"Aye." She bit her lip when his fingertips trailed down the V of her robe, but she didn't protest, didn't stop him. "When nature's left t'divine direction, instead of bein' controlled by men—or women—that's magic."

"Wha' happens when men—or women—try t'control it?" He didn't open her robe. He just traced that V, down between her breasts, then up again. Over and over.

"That's dark magic," she told him, shivering. "And that has its costs."

"The dragon?" Griff's gaze moved up again, to meet hers, questioning. "Was that dark magic?"

"No." She shook her head, vehement. "The Dragon's t'masculine. The lady's t'feminine. All of nature fits together this way—mated."

Fated.

She thought this, but didn't say it. She saw the way he looked at her, the desire in his eyes, and wondered if he saw hers too. There were things in the world that were just meant to fit together.

"Male'n'female," she went on. "Tis like t'guardian 'n 'handmaiden of this temple. Or Ardis'n'Asher. They were true mates."

Griff shook his head, like he was clearing it. "But I do'na b'lieve in—"

"True mates. Aye." She smiled. "But all matin's magical. Magic only helps nature. It can'na do anythin' that nature doesn't intend. That's why all truly *is* as it should be."

"If all is as it should be, then…" He looked at her, a sly smile spreading on his face. "Then I was meant t'best ye this afternoon in our swordplay."

He was trying to bait her, goad her.

"Aye, wulver." Bridget smiled, nodding. "I s'pose that's so."

"If all is as it should be, then I was meant t'come 'ere. An' ye—" He grinned. "Were meant to be kneelin' beside this tub, scrubbing m'back clean."

"A priestess lives t'serve." She wasn't going to let this man win, she decided. Not in this arena, anyway. "The handmaiden offers her gift t'those who're worthy. An' a guardian knows when t'fight… an' when t'yield."

He chuckled, handing her his empty cup. "Ye've a hard time yieldin', lass."

"I'm still learnin'." She smiled, getting up to put their cups and the bottle of wine on the table.

"Mayhaps ye need a new teacher?" Griff grinned when she whirled to glare at him.

"Alaric's been the best teacher'n'father I could've asked fer." She had told herself she wasn't going to let him get to her, but he did. He got under her skin in a way she'd never known before. She didn't understand it.

"I'm sure he has," Griff agreed, picking up the soap and sliding it over his skin. "But e'ery daughter mus' someday leave 'er home fer a mate."

"But I'll never leave this place." She sat on the stool again, watching as the big man stood in the tub, water

- 71 -

sheeting off his body, running down his skin in rivulets. He washed himself with big, soapy hands. She tried to avert her eyes, but she was too transfixed by the man's body. She was surprised she had a voice at all when she murmured, "I've been trained to be the handmaiden'n'guardian, both. Tis m'destiny…"

A destiny she had never questioned before. She'd never had reason to question it. So why did this man, and his ideas, make her doubt?

But he did.

"Tis that what ye want, Bridget?" Griff's hands moved down between his legs, and her gaze went there, too. She flushed, feeling shame at her inability to turn her head, but she could not look away. He held his erection like a sword at the ready, soapy hand moving idly up and down the shaft. She found herself face-to-face with his stiff length. Something that had seemed so small and soft, like a coiled snake, had risen to more than twice that size.

She knew what men did with it—what men and women were meant to do, how they fit together. That thought made the pulse between her own legs throb, hot, insistent.

"I've ne'er questioned it," she breathed.

"Maybe ye should." His hand moved down to cup those sensitive stones men had, the sack underneath taut, soaping them up.

"Why?" She shook her head, heard the pain in her own voice. She didn't like the way he made her think about things. Before he'd come, life had been very simple. Why had he come to complicate things?

"Why not?" he called as she stood, feeling wobbly on her own legs, not sure if it was the wine or the discussion, heading to the fire to get the last rinse bucket.

"Because…" She gulped, lifting the bucket. "Tis all as it should be."

When she turned, seeing him standing in the tub, soap suds sliding down his skin into the bath water, he took her breath away. She didn't understand it. Why should the sight of a naked man make her feel so woozy and warm? Her insides felt soft and gooey, like she was melting. It was the strangest thing she'd ever felt.

Griff met her eyes as she approached, and she wondered if he saw the confusion on her face. He looked at her like he was wondering what she was feeling. She was wondering herself. Slowly, she climbed onto the stool, so they stood face to face, Bridget holding the rinse bucket.

"Tell me, Bridget…" His voice was soft, his gaze too. "If… if somethin', some circumstance, some person… made it impossible for ye to stay 'ere, in this temple…"

She could barely breathe, standing so close to him, and part of her hated him for making her think of these things. The thought of leaving the temple made her stomach clench and her eyes sting. She loved her parents, she loved her home. And this was home. It always would be.

So why was she suddenly filled with such longing?

"If tha' happened…" Griff said. "Then is that as it should be, as well?"

"Ye make m'head hurt." Bridget lifted the bucket and poured it over his head.

Griff sputtered, laughing, rubbing his face clear so he could look at her.

"Too much thinkin'?" he asked, grinning as she climbed down off the stool, setting the bucket aside.

"No, I enjoy thinkin'," she protested, going over to get one of the dry bath sheets warming by the fire. "I play chess wit' Alaric. But tis folly t'question what is. T'would be like askin' yerself why y'er a wulver… and I'm a woman."

"I'm askin' myself that," he said, his gaze skipping down once more to the wet front of her robe. "Righ' this very moment."

"Noticin' an' askin' why're two very different things." She smirked, shaking her head as she unfolded the bath sheet.

"Aye, they are." He agreed, waiting patiently as she untangled the sheet. "Yer wet."

"Pardon?" She blinked at him.

"Yer shift." He nodded, his gaze heavy-lidded. "It's wet. Are ye cold?"

"The fire's warm." It was—but so were her cheeks, and those weren't facing the flame.

"Yer goin' t'need a bath after me." He chuckled as she shook the sheet, holding it out for him.

"I'll be fine." But she wasn't fine. She felt quite strange. Her knees shook.

"Bridget?" Griff tilted his head, frowning, and her face flushed even more.

"I'm fine." She felt it happening, the room spinning, her balance gone.

Griff reached out to grab her by the elbows and she gave a little shriek as she slipped, the stool going out from under her as she fell forward into him, both of them splashing together into the tub. There was nothing else to do, nowhere else to go.

Griff didn't say anything, but he caught her, keeping her head from hitting the other edge of the tub, but unable to keep her from sinking into the water. With both of them in it, the water overflowed the tub's edge, spilling onto the floor in waves.

"Are ye'll righ', lass?" Griff asked, holding her to him as she sputtered and blinked at him in surprise. She found herself stretched out against his naked body in the tub, and when she looked down, she noticed her robe had come untied entirely. Like any Scot, she wore nothing under her plaid—and nothing under her temple robes either.

Griff's eyes flashed as he glimpsed her nude form. Bridget saw them, for just a moment, go from that strange amber to red, the hands gripping her shoulders sliding slowly down her arms as they rocked together in the sloshing water. She didn't need to look down to know what was rubbing up against her hip, hot and hard as steel.

She half expected him to grab her, force himself inside of her—she was a virgin, still, of course, just as she'd told him. There had never been a man, or wulver, here to take her maidenhead. That flash of red in his eyes, and the way his gaze raked her now nude body, his hands moving over her skin, sliding the thin, wet, completely see-through material of her robe down her shoulders, all told her what he wanted.

And she wanted it too.

Her thighs gripped him, hips rocking all on their own. Griff gasped when he felt her shift in his lap, the seam of her sex rubbing against his erection. Bridget gave a little cry, biting her lip, the feel of her breasts flattened hard into his chest reminding her of their sparring that afternoon. This was sparring too, of sorts, wasn't it?

She swiped a strand of wet hair out of her face, trying to regain her composure, which was simply impossible in this situation.

"Well, lass..." Griff's face spread into a grin, hands settling on her hips. "I s'pose all is as it should be now, eh?"

"Yer insufferable." She rolled her eyes, putting her hands against his chest and pushing hard. She would have been too fast for him, if the weight of her wet robe, and the bath sheet that had tangled around her legs, hadn't restrained her. Griff managed to wrap his big arms around her waist, trapping her against him.

"Y'were meant t'fall into m'arms like this, lass," he teased. "It's fate. Destiny, y'ken?"

"M'knee in yer stones is goin' t'be yer destiny in a moment," she snapped and he laughed. But he let her go, and Bridget climbed slowly out of the tub, taking her wet robe and the soaking wet bath sheet with her. The whole room was a mess, water all over the floor.

She shivered, digging another bath sheet out of the bureau and wrapping herself in it. It wasn't fire-warm, but it would do.

"D'ye 'ave another one of those, lass?" Griff called, climbing out of the tub too.

"'Ere…" She tossed it over her shoulder at him, not caring if it fell into all the water on the floor.

"Thank ye." He chuckled.

Bridget glanced back at Griff. He clearly had no qualms about being naked around her, even with an erection the size of Stonehenge. She watched him dry himself in the light of the fire, his back to her, to give her privacy. She found another robe tucked way in the back of the bureau, one of her mother's, and dropped the bath sheet to the floor, slipping the dry robe on and cinching it closed.

Watching Griff dry off—he was far less concerned about exposing himself, and water ran down his back and sides in rivulets as he toweled his long, dark hair—she found herself fascinated by his body. How different from her own. He was lean and muscled, a truly stunning sight. And the way he felt, pressed against her…

Finally, Griff wrapped the sheet around his waist, tucking the material into itself, and asked, "Are ye decent, lass?"

"Aye." She was shivering now, although she didn't feel cold at all. "I did'na mean t'fall in."

"No, I don't expect ye did." He chuckled, surveying the wet floor. "Yer a'righ'?"

"Aye. But I should go change." She sighed, looking at the mess. "I'll come back t'clean up."

"Do'na worry 'bout it, lass." He half-sat on the mattress.

"Are ye sure?" She frowned, nodding at the bed. "Aleesa left ye a tunic t'wear, and a plaid—one of Alaric's. I'll take yer clothes an' we'll wash 'em."

"Ye do'na hafta do that," he said, watching as she made her way through the water. It was already starting to dry in patches, from the heat of the fire. She reached down and picked up her robe, wringing it out over the tub.

"I hafta wash these, anyway," she said with a sigh, wringing out the wet bath sheets too.

"Well, thank ye." He glanced back at the mattress he was leaning against. "T'will be nice t'sleep in a bed tonight."

"Tis Alaric and Aleesa's," she told him, regretting it the moment she said so, seeing the startled look on his face. "They wanted ye t'have it. Because... yer t'red wulver."

He frowned. "But where'll they sleep?"

"We've a room for guests." She smiled as she passed him. "Do'na worry. Sleep well, red wulver."

Griff grabbed her elbow and Bridget gasped. Her feet were still wet and she nearly slipped on the stone floor. Once again, he caught her.

"Will ye stay wit' me, lass?" His eyes searched hers, his voice low and soft, gripping her upper arm. "Keep a man warm?"

"Yer not a man, yer a wulver. And... tis not m'job t'warm yer bed." She glanced down at where he held onto her arm. His whole hand could encircle it. "If I wanted t'share it, ye'd know."

"How would I know?" He let her go, their eyes still locked. He was smiling.

"'Cause I'd be in it." She turned and went to the door, picking up his clothes and boots before opening it and glancing over her shoulder at him. "See ye at breakfast, red wulver. Have a g'nite."

He gave a sigh as she started to close the door, calling out, "G'nite, Bridget."

She stood outside his room for a moment, trying to catch her breath.

She stood there fighting with herself and her own urges.

He'd asked her to come to his bed, and she'd been right to refuse him. She knew that much. It was the right thing to do, for the temple, for her role as both future high priestess and guardian. She'd made the right decision, and she knew both Alaric and Aleesa, who were bedding down at the other end of the long tunnel, would be proud of her.

So why did she feel so empty?

Chapter Five

Griff spent the next three days, until the high moon, avoiding Bridget.

It wasn't that difficult. Aleesa monopolized him at breakfast, wanting to know everything about his den and his pack. She had so many questions about her daughter, Kirstin, and the wulvers Aleesa and Alaric had known. And all those who had come after, too, those she'd never had a chance to know.

After breakfast, Alaric took Bridget out on the horses for training, and while Griff had attempted avoiding that, too, he'd been roped into it both days. Uri needed the exercise, anyway. That's what he told himself, as he found himself facing Bridget in her English-Scottish hybrid armor. Alaric was hellbent on using Griff as a practice dummy for his daughter, and while he'd refused, more than once, Bridget had managed to goad him into fighting.

The first time, he was a gentleman and he let her win— which wasn't easy for him—and then she'd accused him of such. So the second time, he beat her soundly, and she'd accused him of cheating. Could he help it if the girl's body was like a gory damned magnet he found himself drawn to? He hadn't been cheating. He'd just been—distracted.

Before lunch, the women did their purification ritual at the sacred pool. Griff steered clear of that, and Alaric did, too. The older wulver took him out to set snares and check traps. They spent time talking about Griff's father, Raife, and Raife and Darrow's father, Garaith. Of course, they both knew that Garaith was only Raife's father by name only. King Henry VII was Raife's father by blood—the same blood that flowed through Griff's veins.

But while his pack knew the truth, few people outside of Scotland's borderlands, where the wulver den resided, knew that King Henry VII had once bed a wulver woman, let alone that his issue, a warrior who was half-man, half-wolf, led the last pack of wulvers.

But were they the last?

Alaric told him he wasn't sure if their den was the last. The guardian Alaric had slain when Aleesa had first come to the Temple of Ardis and Asher had been a wulver, not a man. But he was not a wulver Alaric knew, and he hadn't had a chance to ask the other warrior where he'd come from. And there was no priestess who resided here then. Aleesa had explained to her husband that she had been called to the temple by the dying high priestess—the wulver woman who had been the slain wulver's mate.

So if there had been two wulvers living here, two wulvers that Alaric and Aleesa did not know—mayhaps there were others, somewhere. There must be, Griff reasoned. They might all be descendants of the first wolf-human union—according to legend, Ardis was a woman, who turned into a wolf during the full moon, and Asher was the human man she loved—but the world was a big place.

He knew this from Rory MacFalon, who studied maps with his father, Donal. Were there wulvers in England? France? Were there wulvers in lands beyond, that they had yet to explore? There were humans in those places—why would there not be wulvers? The thought of traveling to find those lost packs, of joining those wulver forces, excited him beyond words.

He was impatient to find them. Impatient to be off. But he had to wait. According to Alaric and Aleesa, they had to wait for the high moon to read the location of the lost packs in the scrying pool. This annoyed him more than he could say, but he had no choice but to believe what Alaric and Aleesa said.

The truth was, Griff wasn't sure what to believe. He'd dreamed of the dragon both nights, alone in the big bed. The mattress was very comfortable, and while he'd offered to give it up to its rightful owners, the wulver couple had insisted he sleep in their bed. Sometimes he wondered if he'd really seen the dragon rising from the pool, the one he'd been sure was going to attack Bridget when it turned its scaly head, or if he'd dreamed that, too.

The temple had that surreal feel to it. Mayhaps he was really dead and dreaming all of this, he thought sometimes at night, staring up at the shadows on the ceiling, wondering if Bridget was as wide awake as he was at the other end of the cavernous tunnel. Bridget, though, was made of flesh. That he was certain. He had felt it pressed against him more than once. Her flesh seemed to call to him, every moment of the day, in spite of his efforts to avoid her.

It was the most difficult at dinner, when she sat right beside him. He couldn't seem to resist her bait. That little smirk when she saw she'd goaded him into verbally sparring with her drove him mad. He'd noticed Aleesa looking between them, a knowing look on her face. The older wulver woman sensed something. Knew something, mayhaps.

He wasn't sure of it, though, until he overheard them on that third day, talking after the purification ritual as they made rabbit stew for lunch. He had ridden Uri out to the edge of the island—to the sea—and back again. He wanted to make sure that the ship which had brought him into Skara Brae was still anchored there, getting assurance from the captain that yes, they were sailing to another small island that day, but would be there on Skara Brae on the morrow.

Alaric had let him back into the temple at the rock. Rain had soaked Griff to the skin and Alaric sent him in to the kitchen to get dry, telling him he'd rub Uri down and feed him. Griff had meant to announce his presence to the chatting woman—but he'd stopped just outside the kitchen when he heard his name spoken in relation to hers.

"Bridget, ye can'na go wit' Griff," Aleesa told her daughter. "E'en if t'man wanted ye... has he said so?"

Griff stopped, wincing at the way his feet squished in his boots. There was a storm coming in topside, he was sure. He heard Bridget sigh.

"Nay, he's n'said a word." Bridget's voice was small. "But... what if..."

"Bridget, we've spent our whole lives trainin' ye," Aleesa insisted. "I can'na b'lieve he's yer one true mate. Unless... mayhaps... he's meant to be t'guardian 'ere in the temple...?"

Bridget snorted a laugh at that and Griff frowned, stiffening at her laughter. Was it such a strange idea, that he be a protector of this place? Not that it was something he was interested in doing, he had to admit.

"Ye said he's t'red wulver," Bridget reminded her mother. "Even if t'dragon and t'lady did'na confirm it."

"Ye saw him change, as well as I did," Aleesa replied. "I've ne'er seen a red wulver warrior a'fore, and neither has Alaric. He's t'red wulver. And ye saw 'is eyes!"

"Aye," Bridget readily agreed. "But Mother, I... t'way I feel 'bout 'im..."

Griff leaned against the cavern wall, feeling his heart beating hard in his chest at her words. What way did she feel? He wondered. Because for all he could tell, the girl hated him. At least, that was the message she'd been sending since the first time they met. The incident in the tub notwithstanding—and that had been an accident.

The truth was, he wanted to bed her. Bridget was one of the most beautiful women he'd ever seen, with or without clothes, and he wanted her. He would've taken her to bed that first night if she'd agreed. But she'd turned him down. It wasn't a common occurrence for him, he had to admit, but he understood her desire to retain her maidenhood. She was intended to be a priestess here, no different than a nun called to be married to the Lord in a convent, he supposed.

He couldn't say he understood it, exactly, but he could respect it.

So he'd done his best to avoid her. Not that it was easy in such a confined space. And even when they weren't together, in the same room, he could feel her somehow. Her presence was far bigger than her slight form, that was certain. He seemed to carry it with him wherever he went.

"Oh Bridget," Aleesa cried. "I wouldna expect ye t'understand t'ways of men'n'women. Ye've been so sheltered 'ere."

Griff grinned to himself. That was true enough. The girl was definitely a virgin. He'd bedded a few of them, in his time, but he preferred a more experienced woman, given his choice.

"I know what matin' is, Mother." Bridget laughed. "That's… that's not it. I could've mated wit' him if I wanted t'do so. He made that clear enough."

"Bridget!" Aleesa gasped, sounding shocked.

"We've done nothin'," Bridget protested.

Griff heard the lie in her voice, the defensiveness. No, they'd done nothing. Technically, they'd done little more than rub up against one another. But there was something between them, regardless of what physical contact they'd had. He wouldn't have admitted it out loud, either, but he couldn't lie to himself.

"But, Mother, I… I've ne'er felt this way a'fore about someone," Bridget said, lowering her voice, as if someone might overhear. As if her own mind might hear what she was thinking, and her heart take note. He understood that kind of caution, even as he stood in the tunnel and eavesdropped. "I do'na understand it."

Aleesa didn't say anything, and Griff wondered at their silence. He considered making his presence known, glancing behind him into the tunnel, knowing Alaric would be along soon.

"Daughter, listen to me…" Aleesa's voice was low, so low he had to strain to hear it.

"I'm not yer daughter," Bridget whispered.

"Oh aye, ye're m'daughter," Aleesa assured her. "Yer mine, ye've been mine, since the first day I held ye in m'arms and rocked ye t'sleep. I love ye jus' as much as if ye'd come from m'own body, chile."

Griff heard Bridget sniff and he wondered if she was crying. The thought made his chest feel tight, as if something heavy had just sat on it.

"Listen t'me," Aleesa said again. "T'marriage of t'sun'n'moon is due vera soon, y'ken?"

"Aye," Bridget agreed, sniffing again and sighing. "T'marriage of Asher and Ardis. And I'm t'take m'vows as high priestess... which means I'll ne'er leave 'ere again."

The sadness in the young woman's voice broke him. He wanted to save her from it, from the fate of living the rest of her life chanting over pools and talking to invisible dragons. If she would say yes—and up until then, he'd been certain her answer would have been no—he would offer to take her with him. He'd never met a woman like Bridget before, a woman who wore armor, who could hold her own with a sword, who could run almost as fast, mayhaps faster, than he could. He'd never known another woman he thought could be his equal, in or out of bed.

But this one...

She didn't deserve this life. He wanted more for her.

He wanted her.

"Oh, lass, do'na cry... a guardian'll come," Aleesa told her daughter in an urgent, reassuring whisper. "Alaric came fer me. A guardian'll come fer ye, too, Bridget. He'll be called here, jus' as I was."

"Aye." Bridget sighed, long and deep, a sigh so full of regret and longing, he was glad he couldn't see her face. If he had seen her face streaked with tears, those big green eyes filled with them, he didn't know what he might do. He was the strongest man—or wulver—he knew. But the girl's tears made him feel as weak as a bairn. "And Griff'll be leavin' on t'morrow."

Ask me t'stay, lass. He closed his eyes, leaning against the cavern wall, trying to shake the feeling. He wouldn't really stay, if she asked him, would he? Mayhaps not. But if she asked him to take her with him? What then? Would he do so?

He thought he would.

Then Aleesa's words came to him, startling him upright. What did she mean, a guardian would come? They expected some man to arrive here at the temple, to take Alaric's place, like Bridget would take Aleesa's? His lip withdrew from his teeth and he snarled silently at the thought. Just imagining another man showing up at the crossroads, Bridget going out to meet him, made his jaw hurt, he was clenching it so hard.

And the moment she took off her helmet, the moment the man saw her green eyes and that fiery red hair flowing over her shoulders...

"Aye, Griff mus' go fulfill 'is own destiny," Aleesa said. "And 'is destiny isn't yers, lass. I'm sorry fer it. I wish yer feelin's fer 'im lined up wit' yer fate 'ere in th' temple."

"I do'na know what I'm feelin' t'tell t'truth..." Bridget sniffed again.

"I think it's jus' the energy of Ardis'n'Asher yer feelin'—t'lady an' t'dragon. T'marriage time's so close. Ye can'na be blamed fer it. And... he *is* a fine-lookin' man..."

"Mother!" Now it was Bridget's turn to sound shocked, but she giggled.

"Jus' remember," Aleesa warned. "Ye mus' be sure. Tis a lifetime commitment, bein' t'high priestess."

"Aye," Bridget agreed, sounding like the weight of the world was on her shoulders.

Griff wanted nothing more than to lift it and carry it for her, if he could.

But he knew it was impossible.

Aleesa was right about one thing. Even if he didn't believe in destinies and prophecies and all of that, he knew she was right about this—he had his own path, and so did Bridget, and they would have to travel them, alone.

With a sigh and a heavy heart, he ran a hand through his wet hair, put a smile on his face, and went into the kitchen, asking, "What's t'eat? I'm starvin'!"

He didn't know what he'd expected—mayhaps dragon heads again, or ladies with silver eyes—but it wasn't this. He hadn't expected actual writing to show up in the scrying pool, reflecting the moon's light from above. And he hadn't expected how it would be, between him and Bridget, as they stood facing each other across the dark, reflective surface.

Aleesa had fretted, afraid the storm would provide too much cloud cover and prevent the high moon from shining in from above, but the storm had come, as Griff thought it might, while they had spent the afternoon in front of the fire in the kitchen, and it had gone again after dinner.

Before that, Bridget helped Aleesa with some mending while Alaric and Griff sat at the table playing chess. They'd been at it for two days, moving the board to the sideboard when it was meal time, since Alaric had challenged Griff after lunch the first day. The old wulver took forever to make a decision before he moved. Griff was impatient with his strategy, wandering restlessly around the kitchen, snacking idly on boiled eggs and whatever else he could find in the larder before Aleesa chased him out again.

He couldn't avoid Bridget in so small a space. He tried. He skirted around her chair, where she sat sighing and darning socks, complaining about Alaric's tendency to get holes in them. He squatted by the fire to warm his hands, glancing back to see her scowling at him. He returned her scowl with one of his own, growling low in his throat, muttering about the storm forcing him to stay inside and the moon that was taking far too long to come to fruit.

"Are ye always in such a hurry?" Bridget snapped.

Griff raised his eyebrows at her, seeing Aleesa frown at her daughter.

"Yer move!" Alaric called.

Griff stood and went over to the board, taking in the old wulver's move in a glance. Two more moves, mayhaps, and he'd have him in checkmate. It would be all over. Griff moved his bishop, knocking out Alaric's rook.

"Gory hell!" Alaric growled.

"Check." Griff went back over to the fire, squatting down to warm his hands again.

"Do'na worry, Father," Bridget said over her shoulder to Alaric, who grumbled, staring at the board, chin in hand. "He's far too impatient. He's bound t'make a mistake."

"Yer so overconfident." Griff chuckled. "I've got 'im in check."

"*I'm* t'one who's overconfident?" Bridget sniffed, raising her eyebrows, but she smiled back at him. He liked making her smile, in spite of himself.

"Oh damn!" Bridget swore, dropping the needle and thread and holding her finger. A drop of blood appeared on her pale skin.

"Distractible," Alaric grumbled from the table, not looking over.

"Aye." Bridget sighed, agreeing.

"Lemme see." Griff took her hand, holding her finger up in the firelight, and without thinking, he put it into his mouth.

It was a normal, wulver thing to do—a wulver could lick his wounds well in minutes, even bad ones—but Bridget cried out in surprise.

Their eyes locked and she tried to pull away, but he held her fast, tasting her essence against his tongue, salty sweet, intoxicating. It was just a tiny pinprick, a miniscule wound, but he couldn't bear to see her hurt. Slowly, she withdrew her index finger from between his lips, her own slightly parted as she traced the line of his mouth, her gaze never leaving his.

He felt Aleesa watching them, breath held. He felt Alaric's gaze, too. And still, he couldn't look away, couldn't for a moment pretend he wasn't feeling it. He didn't care if her parents were in the room—the woman was his, and he wanted her. The urge to take her was almost uncontrollable. His hands actually shook with the effort it took to hold himself back. His cock was like an iron bar under his plaid, pointing at her like an arrow.

"Does it still hurt?" he asked as she slowly pulled her finger away, putting her hands in her lap. Her breath was shallow, face flushed. He wanted to see the rest of her in the firelight, like he had that first night. He wanted to watch her nipples turn rosy and get hard. He wanted to gaze at the fiery hair between her thighs, to bury his face in her soft wetness.

"I'm a'righ'," Bridget breathed, glancing over and seeing Aleesa's face. Her mother was wide-eyed, looking between them like she'd just seen something that really, truly frightened her. "I... I think I need t'lie down fer a while..."

Bridget stood, her mending falling to the floor, but she paid it no mind.

"Call me t'help wit' supper," Bridget said faintly over her shoulder to her mother, moving past him, heading out of the kitchen.

"Do'na toy wit' her," Aleesa managed after a moment, reaching down to pick up Bridget's mending. Her eyes burned into his. "If y'intend t'leave 'ere after tonight, if y'intend to find t'lost packs... please, Griff, do'na toy wit' her."

"Aye," Griff stood slowly, handing her the sock Bridget had been mending. "I'll be in m'room."

Aleesa gave him a stiff nod, and Griff then retired to his room—their room, really. He stretched out on the bed and thought of Bridget, resting just down the hall from him. He thought about her for what felt like hours, until Aleesa's voice called him for supper.

And Bridget sat silently beside him the whole meal, their hands brushing occasionally, sending sparks through him like lightning.

But Aleesa was right, and he knew it. He had to get through that night, when they could tell him the location of the lost packs, and then he'd be on his way again. He would take Uri and ride back to the ship waiting in the harbor. He would set sail and work his way to wherever he might find his kin, the wulver warriors he would take back to his own den, to show his father, to claim his rightful place as leader.

He'd lost sight of what he was here to do. He'd let himself get distracted by a woman. But he was focused again as he stood across the sacred pool from Bridget. Focused and determined. He kept hold of that focus well, until the moon hit its highest point, until she shone her silver face down into the pool, and Bridget reached her small, trembling hands out, palms up, to him, and whispered, "Mirror me."

He didn't respond, not at first. He wasn't even sure what she'd said, until she repeated it, louder this time, her voice shaking. "Griff... mirror me."

He glanced at Aleesa, at the other end of the pool, her palms up. Alaric stood across from her, doing the same.

"I need ye." Bridget lifted her eyes to his, glinting in the moonlight. "Please, Griff..."

Slowly, he lifted his hands, palms out. They weren't touching, couldn't of course, they were too far away, but he felt her just the same. He felt her skin, her palms small and trembling, touching his own. It wasn't possible, but it was so.

"Griff," she murmured again, giving a little cry. "Oh Griff..."

Oh hell. His mouth went dry. His cock swelled. He felt her little mouth against his, as if he were tasting her sweet lips right that moment. How was it possible? His heart hammered in his chest like he'd been running for miles.

"Y'know I do'na b'lieve in magic, lass," Griff said, his voice far more hoarse than he expected it to be.

"Ye do'na hafta b'lieve," she breathed. "Jus' look."

"What am I watchin' fer? Fey folk? Sprites?" He gave her a smile and saw a flicker of one on her lips. "Magical writin' on t'walls?"

"Aye." She nodded. She was breathing hard. So was he. What was happening? "Writin'... in t'pool..."

"Nothin's happenin'," Griff said. His hands were trembling and he tried to still them.

"Oh aye, tis happenin'," Bridget replied, glancing down into the pool, just briefly. "Look!"

He did, and he saw. There, in the pool, was writing. It rippled and moved with the water, but it was writing. He blinked, trying to clear his vision, but the writing stayed. Then he saw the same words, glowing on the monoliths that lined the walls of the cavern. It was backwards on stone, unreadable, but when it was reflected in the pool, it was quite clear.

If it weren't for those ripples breaking the surface...

"Look a'me, Griff. Look a'me..." Bridget urged. She smiled when he met her eyes, and he saw a hint of silver in them, like the moon. "Aye, that's it... concentrate... focus on me..."

He could only see it out of the corner of his eye, because he was staring at Bridget, but the more they focused on each other, the more still the pool became—and the clearer the writing.

"Aleesa, write it down," Alaric called.

"Aye," the wulver woman agreed. She had pad and ink and was recording the words by the light of a small lamp on her end of the pool.

Griff wanted to look, wanted to read the words for himself, but every time he tried, the pool would ripple again, blurring it all.

"Look t'me," Bridget urged, reaching her hands out, as if doing so would touch him, and somehow, it did. She was over there, all the way across the pool, and yet their hands were pressed, palm to palm. He felt her breath on his face, could smell her sweet scent. Heather and silvermoon. "Can ye feel it?"

He nodded. He could. And for a moment, it actually frightened him.

"Do'na look away!" Bridget insisted, calling for him across the water. Griff's gaze lifted again to hers, saw a flicker of a smile on her face as she caught his attention once more. "Aye, good... concentrate... hold steady..."

Every time he looked away from her, the writing would begin to fade, as if the two of them together were powering the light of the moon itself.

"Tis ridiculous," he muttered, squinting down at the water. "What's it say? Does it give ye t'location of t'lost packs?"

"Aye!" Aleesa assured him. "But I will'na b'able t'write it down if ye do'na concentrate!"

"Madness." Griff grumbled again, but listened to Bridget when she called out to him across the pool.

"Tis ye, Griff," Bridget called to him, her fingers spreading wider, as if she were matching her palms to his. "We've ne'er been able t'see it this clear. Yer t'reason. Yer t'red wulver. Tis yer destiny, Griff."

Her words shook him to the core. For all his talk of not believing in prophecies or destiny, her words moved him. Just an indication that leaving his home and kin to follow this path, to find the lost packs, was the right one for him, filled him with hope and pride. When he'd decided to come to Skara Brae to find this temple, he'd made the fastest, most impetuous decison of his life—at least, it had felt that way once he'd been on the ship. And when he was asking around, trying to find out anything about the temple on Skara Brae. And even when he was at the crossroads with Uri, feeling like an idiot, calling out to no one.

But Bridget had been there. The temple was here. The answers, too, were here. He wasn't ready to admit that prophecies and destiny were real or anything—but he couldn't discount them, either. Not now, not after this.

Griff wanted to look down, to read the words Bridget spoke of, but he didn't. Instead, he looked at her, feeling something he'd never experienced before in his life. He wouldn't have been able to describe it if he tried. Bridget had captured him, with her voice, her presence. She was everything, in that moment. The moon. The sun. The universe.

"Hold me, Griff," she murmured. She spoke with a voice so soft, he shouldn't have been able to hear her, but he did. "Do'na lemme go."

"I've got ye, lass," he whispered. His breath was coming fast, as if he was working hard.

"Oh Griff, I..." She gave another small cry and he felt a sudden surge of energy sing through his whole body. It actually made his knees feel weak, and he almost went to them. "Please, hold on, hold on..."

"Aye, lass." His whole body strained with the effort it took to stay focused. But he wasn't about to stop, to let her go. He wasn't sure if he was carrying her, or she was carrying him, or mayhaps they were carrying something together.

"I've almos' got it all," Aleesa called, sounding hurried, rushed. She was writing as fast as she could.

"Hurry, hurry," Bridget urged her mother. Her voice was breathy, panting, and he knew she was exhausting herself with this, whatever it was they were doing together. Griff's hands trembled, and he realized it wasn't his palms, but hers he was feeling. Her little hands trembling, pressed against his.

Impossible.

"Are ye a'righ', lass?" Griff asked, calling across the pool to her. The images on the water shimmered, as if his voice had shaken it.

"Aye, aye," she gasped, crying out again, as if in pain. "Oh! I can't... I..."

"That's it!" Aleesa announced, looking up in triumph. "I've got it all!"

At that, Bridget collapsed.

Griff had her in his arms, before either Alaric or Aleesa could reach her. She was breathing, but too shallow, eyes still closed, mouth moving as if she was speaking, but no words coming out.

"She's still in the trance," Aleesa murmured, putting a hand on her daughter's forehead. "Go put 'er in our bed. She'll come back t'ye…"

"She'd better," he growled at the wulver woman. Aleesa blinked at him in surprise, and he knew it was his fault this had happened. He'd been the one who wanted to know, who insisted they find out where the lost packs were located.

But how could he have known it would be like this? Of course, what had he expected? Some chanting, herbs being thrown like they did during the purification ritual, mayhaps a map to appear?

He hadn't realized he'd be such a part of things, that Bridget would rely on him so heavily during the ritual. Or that it would take so very much out of her. Griff lifted Bridget in his arms—she weighed hardly anything—and carried her into the tunnel. He ignored Aleesa calling after him. It was full dark, but he followed the light at the end of it, where he passed through the kitchen, the fire burning low. Bridget moaned and her eyes fluttered open briefly as he carried her through.

"Griff?" She half-smiled, putting her arms around his neck, clinging to him. "Ye did'na leave me."

She made his heart break in half.

"Nuh, lass."

He put her down on the bed, head on a pillow. She gave a little cry, reaching for him again, and he let her put her arms around his neck, let her pull him close. He kicked his boots off, resting beside her, feeling her heart beating hard against his, like a little bird's.

"Ye'll be a'righ," he whispered, his lips brushing her hairline, smelling her sweetness. He didn't know if it was true—but he said it anyway. "I should ne'er've asked ye t'do this. I'm sorry, lass. I'm so sorry."

He swallowed, tracing her soft features with his finger. She was so small, like a doll. The most beautiful thing he'd ever seen in his life. He could have stayed there, watching her just breathing, forever.

"Has she spoken?" Aleesa came in, asking after her daughter.

"Aye, briefly." He frowned. "Will she be a'righ'?"

"Oh, aye." Aleesa nodded. "She's just exhausted. It takes a great deal of energy. She jus' needs rest. I'll have Alaric come fetch 'er..."

"No," he snapped, reaching for the coverlet and pulling it over Bridget's still form. "She'll stay 'ere."

"Griff..." Aleesa warned, her eyes widening. "Ye can'na..."

"I'll sleep on t'floor," he told her gruffly, putting a big, heavy arm across Bridget. "But we'll not be movin 'er."

"A'righ'." She sighed. "Call me if ye need anythin'?"

"Aye," he agreed, not taking his eyes off Bridget's sleeping face.

Aleesa moved around the room, straightening, coming over to check on her again, a hand pressed to her forehead.

"She's really gonna be a'righ'?" he asked, meeting Aleesa's concerned gaze.

"Aye, she will, lad." Aleesa gave him a small smile, pressing her hand to his forehead for a moment as well. It was small and cool. He felt warm. "And so will ye, *Righ*."

"*Righ*." He blinked at her, surprised at her use of the Gaelic word for *King*.

"T'once and future king." Aleesa sat beside her daughter, looking at them both, thoughtful. "T'will take me a few hours to decipher all the text, but... d'ye wanna know what I saw in t'pool?"

He hesitated. Of course, he wanted to know—it was what he'd come here to discover. Based on whatever she'd seen, he would set out in the morning in search of his kin.

And he would leave Bridget behind.

That thought made his bones hurt and he looked down at her again, those russet colored lashes still against her pale cheeks, her lips pink, slightly parted, her breath still coming too fast.

Aleesa's hand touched his, the one flat on the mattress beside Bridget, as if the arm over her could protect her from all harm.

"In the mornin'." Griff didn't lift his gaze from Bridget's face. "I think we all need a good night's rest."

"Aye," Aleesa agreed. She leaned over and kissed Bridget's forehead, and then she kissed the back of Griff's hand. "G'nite, lad."

The wulver woman hesitated as she opened the door, glancing back at the couple on the bed. Bridget stirred, mumbling something, and Griff stroked her cheek, whispering to her.

"Griff..." Aleesa cleared her throat. "I... about what I said t'ye, earlier tonight..."

He glanced at her and saw her meaning clearly on her face. She didn't have to worry. He'd never felt more connected to a woman—to anyone—than he did to Bridget in this moment. Did he want her? Aye, he did. More than he'd ever wanted anything. But his feelings for her went far beyond the physical. He would protect her with his own life, from now until the end of days.

"I will'na hurt 'er," he said softly. "I give ye m'word."

Aleesa gave him a nod, closing the door behind her.

Chapter Six

He was hers.

It was a dream, she knew it had to be, but they stood, palm to palm, long cords of rope being wrapped around their wrists—a handfasting. Griff's amber-colored eyes were shining with love, and Bridget felt more whole, complete, than she ever had in her entire life. She knew that feeling, as a temple priestess, of being filled by light, lacking nothing, but this was a different sort of wholeness. This was a mating, of two halves becoming one, a union of souls. Someone spoke in her dream, of dragons and ladies, the marriage of the opposites. She knew the prayers, had studied them her whole life, but they sounded different to her ears as she faced the man she loved, cleaving her life to his...

The man she loved.

Griff.

He was there, facing her across a shimmering pool filled with moonlight. He was there, always there. Protecting her from dragons. Catching her when she fell. Even when she'd pricked her finger, he'd been there to comfort her. She saw nothing but him now. It was as if the man had eclipsed everything else in her life just by his sudden existence in it. Her conscious mind, the one that told her that this was impossible, that their paths had meant to cross only for a moment and then diverge again, turned away from him. But something deeper in her knew the truth.

This man was hers, and she was his. It had been meant to be, since before time had begun its neverending countdown to nothingness again. If everything was as it should be, then her deeper self, the one that called for him in her sleep, the one that longed for his touch, the one that surrendered to her feelings, sought only that which was true.

She'd never realized she wanted something so much until she woke, sobbing, at the loss of it.

And he was there.

"Shhh, lass, ye're a'righ'," he soothed.

She opened her eyes, feeling him stretched out beside her, floating as if they were on a cloud.

And then she remembered. She remembered the ritual at the sacred pool, the way the moon had lit up the words on the reflective surface. She remembered her whole body shaking with the effort to stay still, to concentrate, to keep her mind steady and focused. She remembered Griff's eyes, glowing red, looking straight into and through her.

"Did we find 'em?" she mumbled, trying to sit, but her head felt thick and heavy on her neck. "T'lost packs? Yer kin?"

"Aye," he nodded, putting a big hand in the middle of her chest, pressing her to the bed. "I think so. Aleesa's transcribin' it all."

"Does she need m'help?" Bridget struggled again to rise, but Griff's big paw stayed planted in the middle of her chest.

"Bridget, ye need rest." He frowned down at her, those amber eyes searching her face. "I did'na know it would be so..."

"Tirin'?" She smiled, closing her eyes again for a moment. "Tis like anythin' worth doin' I s'pose... it's a worthy effort. Like makin' love or birthin', mayhaps..."

"Interestin' comparisons." Griff chuckled and she opened her eyes to see him smiling down at her, eyes dancing.

"Why'm I here?" She glanced around, realizing they were in Aleesa and Alaric's room, the one Griff had been staying in since he arrived.

"Because I brought ye here," he said simply. "Because yer mine, Bridget, and I will'na leave ye, ne'er again."

She swallowed, breath caught at his words. She had to still be dreaming. She'd fallen back into unconsciousness, where things like this were possible. But she most definitely wasn't looking up into Griff's concerned face, feeling his warm breath on her cheek, the long, hard stretch of his body against hers. Those things couldn't really be happening.

"But ye hafta find yer kin." She reached up to touch his cheek with trembling fingers, just to make sure she wasn't still dreaming. "What 'bout t'lost packs?"

"I'm meant to lead 'em, Bridget." His face was pained. "But I can'na deny m'feelin's fer ye any longer. I want ye as m'wife. My mate. I wanna take ye from this place, this life. Come wit' me. Be mine."

She stared at him, eyes wide now, fully awake. This was no dream.

Griff was here, holding her, and asking...

"What're y'askin' me?" She struggled to comprehend it. "Ye wan' me t'come wit' ye... to find t'lost packs?"

"Why not?" He smiled. "Ye can handle a sword as good as any man I know and yer a fine horsewoman."

"As good?" she snorted. "Better, I'd wager, than most men *or* wulvers ye know..."

"Aye, aye." He laughed. "I'm glad t'see ye've got yer spark back... I was worried 'bout ye..."

"How long've I been sleepin'?" she asked, frowning.

"Jus' a few hours."

She blinked at him. "And what've ye been doin'?"

"Watchin' ye..."

"If I go wit' ye..." She swallowed, trying to let the thought sink in. "I'll miss t'marriage of Ardis and Asher. The ritual of t'sun'n'moon. I won't become high priestess..."

"But is that what ye want?" Griff asked, lacing his fingers with hers. Just his touch made her melt, gave her so many doubts about the course her life had taken thus far. "I will'na stand in t'way if that's really what ye want, lass. I'll leave righ' now..."

Griff made the move to go, and that's when she knew.

"No!" she cried, grabbing his tunic and pulling him back.

He settled back onto the mattress, looking down at her, smiling.

"I think ye wan' more than this life," he murmured. "More than what ye'd 'ave 'ere in this temple."

"How d'ye know that?" She jutted her chin out, defiant.

"I jus' know." He touched her chin with one finger, still smiling that knowing, arrogant smile. "I know ye, Bridget."

"Ye do'na know me," she said with a shake of her head. "Y'only think ye know me. I'm t'woman ye can'na have. If I gave m'self t'ye, ye'd be gone in t'mornin' wit'out a second thought."

His look darkened, and she saw something in his eyes. They turned dark, from gold to the deepest amber.

"Not wit'out ye," he growled.

"Griff, I can'na leave t'temple," she whispered. And that was the crux of it, truly. Even if she wanted to go with him, how could she? "I can'na leave Aleesa'n'Alaric alone 'ere."

"Can'na...?" His finger moved from her chin, trailing down to the hollow of her throat, his touch melting her. "Or will'na?"

"Ye know, I was left 'ere by someone who wanted me t'be trained as priestess and guardian."

Griff made a face. "Ye do'na know that..."

"But I do," she protested. "Just like ye knew t'come 'ere t'Skara Brae, t'look fer t'lost packs. I know I'm meant t'be 'ere, fer the marriage of Asher'n'Ardis, when the eclipse comes... I can feel it in m'bones."

"Och!" Griff rolled his eyes toward the ceiling. "More magic and rituals?"

"I know ye do'na understand it, but..." Bridget touched his chin, bringing his face around so she could look into his eyes. "Did ye *feel* it?"

He frowned. "What d'ye mean?"

"When ye were looking a'me, across t'pool tonight..." she breathed, remembering, her whole body filled with the memory. "Did ye feel that?"

Griff shook his head, eyes clouded, but then, she saw something. Just a flicker.

And finally, he broke.

"Aye," he whispered. His mouth quivered with his confession. "I felt ye. Ye looked a'me, an' it cracked m'heart wide open, lass."

"Oh Griff..." She felt tears coming to her eyes, knowing how difficult it was for him to admit the truth. She'd felt it, too.

"How can I leave 'ere on t'morrow wit'out ye?" he croaked out, lowering his head to her breast. Bridget stroked his hair, feeling tears slipping down her temples at his words. "It'll be like leavin' m'heart behind."

"Mayhaps..." She swallowed, taking a deep breath. "Mayhaps we're only meant t'have this."

"This?" He lifted his face to look at her in the firelight.

"This moment." She touched his cheek, shifting against him, so they were belly to belly. "Tonight. Now."

"I wan' more," he admitted. "I want ye—I want ye *t'be mine*."

"Aye." She nodded. "I want ye, too..."

She bridged the gap between them, easily, lifting her face and pressing her lips to his. They were soft, warm. But she felt him hesitating, felt his body stiffen, holding back as she ran her hands over his chest, putting them up around his neck.

"Och, we can'na do this," he whispered as they parted, and Bridget slid her soft, bare thigh between his. "I promised yer mother..."

"There are no laws 'ere in this temple or among t'wulvers that say we can'na be joined this way," she reminded him as she rolled toward him on the mattress, pinning him beneath her.

"Nay, but..." Griff protested, moaning when she wiggled her way fully onto him, trapping his erection between them. "Och, lass, if we do this, are ye gonna accuse me of leavin' ye in t'morning...?"

"We hafta follow our destinies," she whispered, sitting up on him in a straddle. "Tis as it should be, always."

He gasped when she unpinned her plaid, pulling it away from her body and tossing it aside. His eyes went from that deep, dark, amber color to a rich, bright red when she pulled her tunic off over her head and threw that aside too.

"Always as it should be, eh?" he asked, as Bridget took his hands in hers, putting them at her waist. His hands moved over her skin and she shivered.

"Always," she agreed with a nod, moving her hips, feeling his shaft against the seam of her sex through his plaid.

"Then I should be doin' this...?" His hands moved up to cup her breasts. They were full and ripe, never touched, and he plucked at her nipples like little cherries.

"Oh, aye..." Bridget breathed, rocking faster.

"And this...?" One hand slipped up behind her head and pulled her down to him for a kiss. This was no soft, hesitant thing, but something hard, hot, demanding. His tongue stroked and tickled the roof of her mouth, caressed the velvet walls of her cheeks from the inside, and Bridget looked at him with glazed, lust filled eyes as they parted.

"Oh, aye, aye, definitely that..." She nodded eagerly, wanting more, aching for something, although she wasn't quite sure what.

"And this?" His mouth moved down to capture her nipple, suckling like a babe, and Bridget almost sobbed at the sensation.

"Aye, aye," she cried as Griff rolled her to her back.

She ran her hands over him, greedy, mapping his chest and belly with her palms, memorizing every glorious inch of him. She hadn't been able to get the image of his nude body out of her mind, and now she drank him in as he knelt up to divest himself of tunic and plaid, and she saw him again, stripped bare for her.

"Please, please," she begged him, reaching for the part of him she hadn't dared touch the other day. "I want ye inside me."

Griff hissed through his teeth when she squeezed him, a sound that filled Bridgit with an incredible, feminine power.

"Not yet, lass." He gave a low groan as he leaned over to kiss her and she felt the full weight of him crushing her against the mattress. She gasped and reveled in it, rocking up, wanting more.

"Please," she begged, but that would be just the start to her pleas.

Griff spent eons—it was at least that long, she was sure—kissing and touching her body. He explored every inch of her, from nose to navel, front and back, with fingers, then tongue. She felt like a newborn kitten being given a bath, and all the while, she begged him for more.

Please, Griff, please...

She didn't even know anymore what she wanted, what it was she was asking for.

Then his mouth went lower. He skipped her sex and went to her thighs, rubbing his whiskers there until she was red and raw. Then he turned her over and did the same to her bottom. Her cheeks—the ones on her face—were just as red when he finally rolled her to her back, pushing her knees to her chest, and burying his face in her sex.

"Griff!" Bridget nearly screamed. She bit her lip, remembering Alaric and Aleesa might hear, but soon she forgot all about them. She forgot everything as he pressed his tongue between her aching, swollen lips, flicking a spot at the top of her cleft that made her shake all over when he did.

And then, something happened.

One moment she was trembling all over, crying out as if in pain—because whatever he was doing with his mouth and tongue down there was pure, blissful torture—and then, she flew, or jumped, or mayhaps was pushed, over a shuddering, delicious precipice.

Her hips bucked up off the mattress, her hands reached for something to hold onto, sure she was tumbling, falling, flying, and Griff let her grab his hands. Squeezing them hard, she felt her sex contracting, squeezing too, again and again, quivering waves crashing through her, an ocean of them, all at once.

"What was that?" she asked in wonder, and Griff came up to kiss her.

He tasted strange, musky, and she realized that was how she must taste.

"This may hurt, lass," he whispered, and she felt him at her entrance, pressing slowly.

Oh, it was big!

Bridget cried out as her sex opened to him, the first painful stretch, a slight burn. She put her arms around his neck, clinging to him, and he held her, holding still, waiting. He was inside her now, she felt him, completely filling her. He kissed her, soft, slow. His mouth was entrancing, drawing her out, drawing her against him.

She felt herself untensing, her body unfurling, opening to him.

Then, slowly, he began to move.

"Oh! Griff!" His movements were easy, practiced. She had a moment to wonder if he'd done this before—how many times, with how many other women—but when she looked up into his eyes and saw the light there, she didn't care anymore.

He was hers. In that moment, he was hers. That was all that mattered.

"Och, Bridget," he cried, hips moving faster, rocking into her pelvis, the two of them moving together, like water, flowing over one another.

"Aye," she breathed, meeting him. It was like a dance, a beautiful, perfect dance. "Aye, Griff, oh, aye! Do'na stop!"

He groaned at that, driving her into the mattress with such fury she could scarce draw a breath, not that she cared. Bridget felt it again, that delicious tickle building up to a glorious climax. His shaft created such heat, such friction, everything between them was on fire.

"Look a'me, lass," he whispered, holding himself above her as he thrust. His eyes were pure fire and she cried out as the feeling washed through her again, her sex clamping down on his length. "Och! Bridget!"

He gave one last, hard, thrust, burying himself deep in her womb, and she felt the first wave of his pleasure flowing into her. She clasped him to her, and they rolled, breathless, on the bed, until they were wrapped up together in the coverlet.

When he asked if she regretted what they'd done, she laughed.

"I won't e'er regret that," she murmured against his neck. "Not if I died t'morrow."

"Come wit' me," he asked her again.

But she knew she couldn't. They had this, now, and that was all.

"Ye can'na stay?" she asked him. Griff sighed, and she knew.

They had to follow their paths, each their own.

She didn't know how many times they made love. She lost count. And still, she clung to him, wanting more. If this was all they had, this one night, then she wanted it to last a lifetime in her memory.

But they didn't just make love. They talked. They laughed. They fed each other fruit and drank wine and told each other stories. Bridget told him about the time Alaric thought she'd drowned in the sacred pool—when she'd really been hiding among the rocks. Griff told her about the time his aunt, Laina—Darrow's mate—had turned into she-wolf form and had nearly eaten him when he crept up on her while she was sleeping.

"Surely she would n'have hurt ye?" Bridgit asked, shocked at the thought.

"Wulver women can'na control their cycles." Griff sighed. "E'en their own bairns aren't always safe 'round 'em during their moon time. T'other wulver women take the bairns, and they go somewhere during their moon blood, away from t'pack."

"That's... terrible." Bridgit shuddered. She knew her own mother and father locked themselves in their room—this very room, in fact—during Aleesa's moon cycle. Now she knew why. She couldn't imagine not being in control of your own body in that way. As a human woman, bleeding once a month was bad enough. But turning into a wolf, and not being able to turn back until your moon time was over? Not knowing if you might do something to someone you cared about?

"T'be fair, I should'na been where I was," Griff replied with a shrug. "T'would've been m'own fault if she'd torn m'throat out."

Bridget shook her head, sighing. Even so, she couldn't imagine. Poor Laina—what if such a thing had happened, and she came back knowing she'd done something so awful?

"So, d'ye still think e'erythin's always as it should be?" Griff asked, raising an eyebrow at her.

"I can'na explain t'terrible things that 'appen in t'world," she admitted. "I do'na know t'reason fer 'em. But sometimes ye jus' have t'accept what is."

Griff snorted. "Ye sound like m'father."

"He's a wise man."

Griff snorted at that, too, rolling her over to spank her bottom, just once, making her cry out and laugh at him.

"Ye can'na spank t'truth out," she teased.

"No?" His eyes flashed red as he leapt for her, pouncing, making her giggle and thrash underneath him. "Mayhaps I can do somethin' else t'ye 'til ye forget..."

His hand reached between them to cup her sex and she moaned. She was sore there, they'd been together so many times, but she rocked up against him anyway.

She realized, when he slid inside her again, that although they only had this one night to be together, she'd never get enough of him.

Even if they had a lifetime.

"I thought we might find ye 'ere." Aleesa knelt down beside Bridget at the scrying pool.

"I jus' wanted to watch him go..." Bridget kept the tremble from her voice and was proud of herself for doing it.

She didn't want to tell them they'd already said goodbye. Watching Griff ride away to the south, she felt as if she was watching her future get smaller and smaller in the distance.

"He's a mighty warrior." Aleesa stroked her daughter's hair. "I b'lieve he'll lead t'packs, like t'prophecy says."

Bridget said nothing, just hugged her knees to her chest and rocked, watching him disappear from her life. The scrying pool could only see up to the horizon, and Griff was almost out of sight.

"Aleesa...!" Alaric said his mate's name with alarm, staring into the pool at the other end.

"What is it?" she asked, frowning.

"Riders from t'north." The gray-haired wulver pointed into the pool, peering more closely. "Wulvers... I think... tis Raife."

"Raife?" Bridget's head came up at the sound of Griff's father's name. The man had come after his son? How had he known he would be there?

"I'll saddle up an' go meet 'em." Alaric was already heading toward the exit.

"I wanna come!" Bridget called, jumping up, thinking of meeting Griff's father.

Any way to stay connected with him...

Then a sudden motion in the pool at her feet caught her eye and she stopped, staring at the sight unfolding before her. Bridget cried out, dropping to her knees, peering into the pool, her nose so close, it almost touched the water.

"What is it?" Aleesa looked over the edge and saw, too, her eyes going wide with alarm.

"Griff!" Bridget cried, and then Alaric was there beside her, all three of them watching the events unfold in the scrying pool, unable to do anything but witness the scene.

Griff had been intercepted by a massive band of both men and wulvers.

Not the party approaching from the north, but another one coming in from the south. They were being led by a man—not a wulver, at least, not that Bridget could tell—who yelled orders to men and wulver alike as they surrounded Griff on his horse. They could hear no words, of course—they could only watch.

"No," Bridget whispered, her heart dropping to her toes as she saw how outnumbered he was. What in the world could they want of him?

Suddenly, Griff's horse bolted. He urged it forward, through the mass of wulvers and men, and just as suddenly as it had happened, it was over. They were out of sight of the scrying pool's reach. The water was clear again.

"I'll go after 'im." Alaric's voice was hoarse as he turned to go, but Bridget was up again in a flash, grabbing her father's arm.

"No, I'll go," she insisted. "You mus' ride out an' meet t'wulvers coming from t'north. They know who ye are, they'll trust ye an' follow ye. Ye must bring 'em t'help Griff."

"Aye." Alaric hesitated, brow knit, torn. "But I do'na wan' ye t' go anywhere, lass. Ye stay 'ere wit' yer mother."

"That's not what ye trained me fer." Bridgit drew herself up to her full height, eyes flashing. "I'll follow an' track 'em. I promise, I will'na get t'close."

"Jus' track 'em, lass," he warned, shaking a finger at her. "Leave a trail fer us t'follow."

"Aye, I will." She nodded, her heart already beating hard in her throat.

Aleesa put her arms around her daughter and Bridget let herself take comfort, for just a moment.

"Mother..." she whispered, thinking of Griff, of him in danger, and couldn't bear it.

"T'prophecy says days'll be dark before t'Blood Reign of t'Red Wulver." Aleesa kissed her daughter's forehead softly. "Nothing's certain. Fate'll 'ave its way."

"All is as it should be?" Bridget whispered.

Aleesa nodded, but her eyes were cloudy. "I hope so..."

Chapter Seven

If he hadn't been thinking so much about leaving Bridget, he might have seen them coming. He should have at least smelled them—a few hundred wulvers and men— but he was lost in thought. He cursed himself for it later, of course, being just as moony as Rory over Maire or Garaith over Eilis. He'd never been one to moon about over some female, but instead of tearing over the hills of Skara Brae to meet the ship that would take him to the mainland, he was plodding along, heart heavy. The further he got from the temple, the slower he seemed to go. Uri, impatient with his master's pace, had tried several times to pick it up, but Griff had reined him in.

It was as if there was an invisible string tied from him to the temple—nay, to the lass, Bridget—and it grew more and more taut as he distanced himself. He had to admit, he was daydreaming. He was remembering the press of her full body against his, the creamy expanse of her thighs, the soft press of her lips. Not to mention how quickly lightning flashed in those sea-green eyes. The memory of the way she'd fought him as the guardian, how she'd rallied and come back again and again, made him smile. Little spitfire.

He had left his den to find the lost packs, had traveled to the temple with only that goal in mind. He had been ready for talk of prophecy and magic—he'd lived with it his whole life—but what he hadn't expected was Bridget. All the hoopla about fate and destiny had always seemed silly to him. He didn't like to think of God like some puppet master pulling strings above their heads, making them dance to an old man's tune. Then Bridget's words, "It is all as it should be," kept echoing in his head.

Why had he left his den and come here? Had it been to find the lost packs? Or had the divine had a larger purpose in mind? Had he really traveled all this way just to find his one true mate? To find the red-haired, bright-eyed, saucy little Bridget?

I don't believe in true mates, he reminded himself, glancing back over his shoulder. He could barely see the crossroads and the outcropping where the temple lay. He'd come that far, too far. *I don't believe in true mates, or prophecies, or destiny.*

But how could he say that now, having seen everything Bridget had shown him behind the temple walls? Moonlight and magic, dragons and ladies, had any of it been real? Certainly the way she'd fallen into his arms that night in the tub had been real. And then, when they'd been together the night before... He imagined he could still taste her lips, feel her breath in his ear, smell the sweet, light scent of her skin.

He was lost in his own thoughts when he reached the top of the last hill as he neared the sea. He was distracted, consumed by his own fears and doubts, and they had surrounded him before he knew what was happening. There were a dozen, at least, not just humans, but wulvers as well—wulvers he'd never seen before. They were no kin he knew. The sight startled him even more than the attack itself—wulver warriors he didn't recognize circling him and his horse, mixed with human men wearing armor and carrying swords.

Griff assessed the situation, scanning the line of soldiers, finding its leader—a man wearing dark armor, face plate up, shouting orders to men and wulver alike—and finding its weakness. There was a small break in their line. It wasn't much, but it might be enough. If he was fast.

Years of training took over. Griff made a noise in his throat, digging the heels of his boots into Uri's side, and the horse practically sighed with relief, taking off from a standstill to a run so fast, Griff had to choke up on the reins to keep from being thrown. Uri fled, letting Griff guide him, just as he'd planned, through the small break in his attackers' line. The horse, who had been clearly annoyed with Griff's plodding pace, was relieved to be running again. He had a great deal of pent-up energy, after spending too much time down in the cavern, penned up, and Griff used that to his advantage.

If he'd been home, if it had been their forest, escape wouldn't have been a question. Griff would have easily avoided the attackers at home, but this was Skara Brae, and he didn't know enough about the land and the terrain to lose them. He realized this as he found himself on the rocky beach, the horse struggling in the sand and rocks. A dead end. They could go no further, and there was no ship here to meet them and likely wouldn't be for another hour, mayhaps two. He had left early because if he hadn't left, he knew he would have stayed.

But there was another ship here, and Griff narrowed his eyes at it, seeing the mark on the side, along with a dragon's head. Is this what had carried the men and horses who were after him?

Griff turned Uri so they were galloping along the shoreline, leaning over the neck of his horse, a plan formulating in his head. If he could double back, get to the temple, mayhaps...

Uri tripped. It wasn't the horse's fault. He was used to running in the forest, over the rolling, green hills of home, not on this craggy, rocky beach. His hoof sank into an unseen hole in the sand, and he went down with a shrill, horrible scream.

His leg, it's his leg. The thought of having to put Uri down made Griff far sicker to his stomach than the sound of the approaching horsemen.

They were surrounded again. Griff's side ached—he was wearing full gear again, but the horse had thrown him a good three feet, and his face had been scraped on the rock, along with the rest of him. He tasted blood in his throat as he rolled, reaching for his blade, but it was too late. Three wulver warriors, fully turned, were already off their horses, on him with a net and ropes. Griff shifted. With a shake of his dark head, he shifted, growling and snapping at his attackers. But they were wulvers. They knew exactly what to look out for. The first thing they did was snap on a muzzle, which just made Griff struggle and fight harder.

He almost freed himself, even though it was now six—three men, three wulvers—against one, but then they bound his arms behind his back and chained him.

The only good thing about the entire situation was that Uri's fall hadn't seemed to break anything. The big animal was back up, and one of the wulvers had corralled him, grabbing his reins to lead the horse over the rocks. Griff howled—still in wulver form—when they slung him over the saddle of his horse. His arms were still bound behind him as they lashed him to the saddle and pulled the horse along the beach. Griff struggled, but his kidnappers had tied him well.

They led the horse back up the hill, away from the sea. Griff turned his head, trying to identify any of his kind. He scanned each man, looking for their leader—he remembered the dark knight who had been screaming orders at his men, all of them involving capturing Griff. But why?

"So this is the one." A smooth voice spoke from near the front of the horse, followed by a low, amused chuckle. Griff felt Uri pull instinctively away, the horse giving a nervous whinny, and Griff knew how he felt. His hackles rose at the sound of the man's voice, and he knew, even without seeing him, that this was the man in charge of this little venture. This man, whoever he was, had a purpose in capturing Griff, and whatever it was, it wasn't good.

I won't lead them to the temple. It was the only thing he could imagine they might be searching for. Mayhaps they had already attempted entrance, but had been turned away as unworthy. Bridget had told him, it had happened before. Only certain seekers were even entertained for entrance. Some were judged too dangerous or just plain unworthy, and their cries for entrance went unanswered. Mayhaps these men and wulvers—he couldn't understand how or why his brothers, his kin, for they had to be, if they were his kind, could do this—had already been turned away from the temple, and they had captured him in the hopes he could lead them in.

"I'm not impressed." The man sneered and Griff lifted his wolf head to see the dark knight approaching. He wasn't a Scot. At least, he didn't speak as one. And his armor was definitely English. So what was this shasennach doing with wulvers Griff had never seen before? "Are you sure he's the one?"

"He's wulver," one of the other wulvers confirmed. "And he was comin' from the temple."

So it was the temple, then. Griff felt his limbs go cold at the thought of this band of assailants invading the Temple of Ardis and Asher. He might not believe in the divine and sacred in the same way as the guardians and priestesses who resided there, but he had respect for it. Besides, he would take the information to the grave, if it meant protecting Alaric, Aleesa, and especially Bridget.

Bridget... The young woman's face swam before his eyes. All the blood was rushing to his head at this angle and he lifted it, taking in great gulps of air, determined now to find a way out of this. Not even for himself, or his family, or the lost packs. He just wanted to make sure Bridget remained safe, now and forever.

"Take him down," the man in dark armor instructed. "Off the horse."

The wulvers turned Griff around to the knight, who had taken off his helmet and held it lightly under one arm, his sword in the other. The man was handsome, well-groomed, young—probably Griff's age—and from his accent, quite English. Griff tried to place him. Someone who had visited Castle MacFalon mayhaps? If he could figure out who the man was, he might be able to figure out why the man wanted him.

"You have no earthly idea who I am, do you?" The other man chuckled, flashing a brilliant smile. His blonde hair fell over one eye as he dipped his head to look at Griff, searching his eyes behind the muzzle. "Hm. Where are those fabled red eyes of yours, wulver? Show me."

So that was it, then. The man knew he was the red wulver. Griff just glared at him, working hard not to show him the color of his eyes, because anger rose in him like a coming storm. He shook his head, changing back to human form in an instant, knowing it would be easier to control his emotions this way.

"No?" The man frowned, angry at Griff's resistance, but curious now that he'd changed back into human form. "Mayhaps this will change your mind, then..."

The armored man brought his sword hilt up against the underside of Griff's chin. The blow knocked his head back and he groaned, feeling his teeth rattle in his head as he went to his knees. He gagged, feeling light headed and nauseous, knowing he'd be lucky if he could talk at all for a while after that hit—luckily, he was a wulver and could heal relatively quickly.

"How about now?" the man asked gently, squatting down beside him and lifting Griff's head by the hair.

He snarled at the man, but didn't speak. Griff wasn't about to tell him anything.

"I have a secret to tell you." The other man's eyes were blue—dancing, dazzling blue. "You're not who you think you are."

Griff didn't answer him. He didn't care who this man thought he was. All he could think of was how he could protect Bridget from these marauders. If that meant letting them take him, then that's what he'd have to do. The thought of killing all of them was certainly his first choice, though.

"Should I introduce myself, little doggie?" The man's cruel slice of a mouth spread into a grin. "My name is Uldred Lothienne. Does that sound familiar to you?"

It did, although at first, Griff couldn't think why. He could hardly think at all, the way his ears were still ringing.

But then he remembered the story his mother and aunts had told him when he was a pup.

"Ah, I see you have heard of me. Or, at least, my father before me." Uldred laughed, an overloud sound that brought light, nervous chuckles from his men. "Can you guess who my mother is, little pup? I'll give you three."

Griff wasn't playing games. He focused on trying to breathe—and in the midst of basic bodily functions, to think. Eldred Lothienne's son. King Henry VII's royal huntsman had always hated wulvers, had made it his mission to kill them all—after his consort, the witch Moraga, had used her magic to enslave the wulver warriors to do his bidding. Which, of course, had involved usurping the English king's throne.

He'd heard the story a hundred times, from Donal MacFalon himself, who had slain Lord Lothienne and thwarted his plan to become king of all England. And he knew, too, that the witch Moraga was the reason that no wulver could ever go back to their mountain den. She'd gone missing after being captured—according to rumor, she'd been locked in a cell, but had simply disappeared.

Darrow, just as skeptical as Griff, believed someone had let the evil woman go, and he had a tendency to believe this, more than he believed the witch had said some magic words and spirited herself away. As far as he knew, the woman hadn't been heard from again—both his father, Raife, and Donal MacFalon, had sent many men out to find her over the years—and most assumed her dead.

Griff's mother, Sibyl, spoke of returning to their mountain den often, but Raife wouldn't allow it. Griff thought it was ridiculous to keep their growing pack confined to such small quarters, when a much bigger, ready-made home sat empty, but now he wondered if his father might have been right. Was this English knight really the issue of the bewitching Moraga and the devious wulver-hating Lord Eldred Lothienne?

Because, if he was a guessing sort of man, Griff definitely would have guessed that Uldred was their son.

"No guesses?" Uldred's brows drew together in consternation. "What kind of fun is it, if you don't guess?"

Griff managed not to pass out, but just barely, when the other man hit him upside the head with the hilt of his sword. The world went black for a moment, and he heard the man's voice, but not the words he was saying. It took him a moment to tune back in.

"...as stupid as you look! My mother is the witch Moraga. Look at me!" Uldred grabbed Griff by the top of the head again, jerking his face up so Uldred could yell into it. "I have spent my entire life waiting for the time I could avenge my father's death—but I intend to do far more than that."

Griff knew his pack was in danger. He'd left them alone, undefended, with this madman on the loose. He couldn't have known, but that didn't matter. His mother, his aunts, his sisters—and the entire MacFalon clan. Because it had been Donal MacFalon who had slain Lord Lothienne, who had tied the half-dead man to his horse and dragged him behind until he was all the way dead. It's what Lothienne and men like him had done to wulvers for centuries, a fitting end to a cruel, devious man's life.

But Griff didn't think his son would see it that way.

So what was the younger Lothienne doing here, on Skara Brae? Griff had clearly been followed. So they wanted him, mayhaps to draw the other wulvers out, mayhaps to use him to find the den.

If they didn't already know where it was.

If his family wasn't already dead.

Oh God, that couldn't be true. He wouldn't let that be true.

"You see, my poor, sad, misguided, little puppy..." Uldred's hand moved through Griff's hair like he was petting him, a smile stretching the man's thin lips even thinner. He moved close, and whispered in Griff's still ringing ear, so that his men did not hear. "You're not the red wulver... I am."

Griff jerked his head away from the man's touch, hearing him laugh, a low, grating sound. If this man was a wulver, then he was a pig—and while Griff had a hearty appetite and occasionally found himself rolling in the mud, he definitely didn't have a snout or say "oink."

"Oh, I'm not yet." Uldred tapped Griff's cheek lightly a few times with a gloved hand. "But I will be. My mother... you've heard of my mother, the witch, Moraga, have you not? She's more powerful now than she was even then. And she wants me to take my rightful place, among men *and* wulvers."

Rightful place? Griff sneered. Did this fool really believe he could lead a pack of men, let alone wulvers? No wulvers he knew would follow him. Which made Griff look both left and right at the wulvers on either side, who held his chains. Who were these dogs? Where had they come from? They weren't part of his pack—and no wulver he'd ever known would serve a Lothienne, even for the promise of gold. Wulvers were loyal, honorable.

They're being compelled.

This thought flitted briefly across Griff's mind and he wondered if it was true. That had been part of the story, hadn't it? He tried to remember what he'd heard about the witch, Moraga, and her plan to enslave the wulvers for her consort, Lord Eldred. At the time, it had seemed ridiculous, of course. The thought that some woman could compel an entire den of wulver warriors to fight for this man was insanity.

The stories he'd heard as a pup, back in his den, were that Eldred Lothienne and the witch Moraga had planned to enslave all of the wulver warriors to use them to take the throne—and then have them turn on one another until there were no more wulvers left on Earth. The witch claimed all she needed was the wulver leader's blood—Griff's father, Raife, had been the wulver leader at the time—and she'd almost gotten it, too. Griff didn't know if it was still Raife she needed. Mayhaps Raife's son, Griff, would do?

Was that why he was being taken?

Uldred leaned in close enough that Griff felt the man's hot breath on his cheek. "You see, I don't need to actually *be* the red wulver—I just need them to believe that I am. Then I can reunite all of the lost packs, and use them all to take the throne. And with your blood, I can enslave them—forever."

Griff's stomach dropped. He knew about the lost packs. Uldred was using the prophecy, using it against the wulvers. But how could he have convinced these wulvers that he was the red wulver? The man couldn't shift. His eyes did not glow red. Unless, some magic...?

Griff would have said he didn't believe in magic before entering the Temple of Ardis and Asher, but after what he'd gone through with Bridget at the sacred pool, he wasn't so sure. They'd only touched briefly on the idea of "dark magic," but he wondered at it, because that was the kind of magic Uldred and his mother, Moraga, would be entertaining. Something foul, and unnatural.

Is that what they had planned?

"And if the prophecy is real?" Uldred was still speaking just to him, his tone gleeful. "Oh, I do so hope the prophecy is real, as my mother believes. You see, we share an ancestor, you and I, one that you can trace back to Asher and Ardis, as you wulvers call them—but we knew him as Arthur. The king who pulled the sword from the stone? Thanks to Merlin, who decided it was wise to teach his pupil by turning him into animals, we may not share a mother and father, but we are blood brothers, after a fashion. And I need yours."

"For what?" Griff snarled. To turn his wulver brothers against him? To compel them to follow this man, whose ravings were just simply mad?

"If the prophecy is real, when I look into the pool at the Temple of Ardis and Asher during the eclipse, *I will become the red wulver,*" Uldred told him, his blue eyes dancing wildly. "And if it's all nonsense—well, then, I'll have your blood, and my mother can use it to compel the wulvers anyway."

Griff's blood ran cold at the thought.

"The eclipse is coming. The prophecy is at hand." Uldred tilted Griff's head up toward the sky, searching his face. He knew the man was looking for a flash of red, some sign that he'd grabbed the right wulver. His voice rang out louder. The men were listening. "The red wulver will unite the lost packs and become far greater than any king of England. The red wulver will become the Dragon King of the Blood Reign. And I am that wulver!"

Did the man really believe the wulvers would think he was one of them? Griff couldn't believe it, but the three wulvers around him howled, and then took a knee, as if Uldred was their rightful king. He could smell this fakery from a mile away. Why could they not?

Before Griff could think more on it, Uldred leaned back in to tell him something only for his ears.

"I may still need Raife's blood, but your father's on his way right now to bring his pup home. Then I will be able to control all the wulvers. Even you, pet."

"Over m'dead body." Griff growled, throwing himself forward toward the man, yanking the chain taut as Uldred stood, laughing at Griff's impotent display.

"That's a possibility." Uldred shrugged, glancing to his men. "Any wulvers who do not follow me will certainly die. I'm getting to the end of my patience with this one."

Griff howled when Uldred nodded at his men and they brought forth a wulver whose face had been beaten bloody, almost beyond recognition. Not that Griff needed eyesight to know his friend, Rory MacFalon, also in chains.

"Let 'im go," Griff croaked. How had they captured Rory? What had they done to him? Of course they would capture The MacFalon's son.

And now Griff's father, Raife, and, he imagined, Darrow and the rest of the wulver warriors, were on their way to Skara Brae, and were about to walk right into Uldred's trap. Griff felt his rage rising, felt the heat in his eyes, and knew they were turning red. He couldn't stop it.

"They'll ne'er follow ye!" Griff snapped at Uldred as Rory lifted his head, giving a low moan.

Griff shook his head, his snout filling the muzzle they'd put on him as he howled, his eyes burning as he looked around at the wulvers. Not just the ones who held his chains, or the ones who held Rory's, but there were more, still, wulvers who had joined this man's ranks. Were these part of the lost packs? Had they believed Uldred when he told them he was the red wulver?

"They'll only e'er follow t'red wulver, t'one true king!" Griff roared, yanking to the ends of his chains, snapping at the dark knight, in spite of the muzzle, frothing at the mouth. His voice rose into a long, keening wail, and to his surprise, several other wulvers responded in kind, throwing their heads back and howling.

For one brief moment, Griff had hope. Did they recognize his voice? Did they see him as the red wulver? One of the wulver guards who held his chains saw Griff's eyes flash red. Griff saw some sort of reaction—surprise? Recognition? He wasn't sure.

"Shut up, dog!" Uldred roared, bringing the hilt of his sword back around again at Griff's head. "*I am the one true king!*"

That was the last thing Griff heard before he hit the ground and sank into darkness.

⚜

Griff woke in a cage. A wulver's worst nightmare.

His sword was gone. He'd been stripped down to tunic and plaid, and not only was the cage made of thick, iron bars, but he was chained to it, too. His first memory was seeing Rory MacFalon, bloody and beaten almost unrecognizable, and he looked around, hoping to find his friend. Mayhaps, together, they could form some sort of plan to escape.

But he was alone. Chained inside a cage, inside a tent. They'd had time to put up a tent? Mayhaps, then, they hadn't found the temple yet. He could only hope. He had to get back and warn them. The thought of Bridget in danger made him crazy with anger and he moved to the front of the cage, testing the bars. Solid. There was a padlock keeping the cage door closed. He saw this by the light of a small lamp lit in the corner on a low table.

Griff shook his head, changing to half-man, half-wolf form, and then cocked his head, listening. He could hear far more like this. There were wulvers and men, and not just a few. Dozens. Maybe even a hundred or more. His tent wasn't the only one that had been set up. One conversation was close. A human and a wulver, standing outside the tent. Guards. They were talking about a dice game, amiably arguing over winnings. Distractible. That was good.

He knew it was likely useless but he had to try. Griff grabbed a hold of the bars and pulled. They didn't budge. Uldred knew enough about wulvers to know how to contain them. Griff knew he would likely be able to snap the chain, but the cage, that was going to be a problem. He'd have to work on the lock.

"Stand in the presence of your once and future king!" Uldred's voice carried in to him, even though the flap of the tent was closed.

Griff felt a growl growing in his throat, unbidden. He worked hard to control it, holding onto the bars and leaning in to listen. The wulver and the man mumbled apologies. Anyone else would have heard nothing but contrition, but Griff knew wulvers. This one was acting contrite, but mayhaps wasn't feeling that way. He heard a resistance in the wulver's tone, and that was heartening.

"Ye heard 'im!" A woman's voice snapped, clearly Scottish. "Take a knee before yer king!"

His spine straightened at the sound. Moraga. He didn't know, not for sure, but who else?

"Don't tease the animals, Mother." Uldred chuckled as he opened the tent flap and stepped inside. Griff snarled at him, and at the woman who followed him into the tent.

"So this is t'red wulver." The blonde who approached the cage surprised him. He'd expected a witch—an old woman, wrinkled and bent. This woman was tall, voluptuous, her blonde hair thick and long down her back. She spoke like a Scotswoman but she dressed like a shasennach.

"Not so loud, Mother," Uldred hissed, glancing toward the tent entrance. "Don't tempt fate. The other wulvers are already doubting and restless."

"They won't be fer long." Moraga swung her hips, moving toward the cage. "I've ne'er seen one wit' red fur…"

"Guess that's why they call him the red wulver." Uldred crossed his arms, glowering at Griff. "Fools."

"An' ye saw 'is red eyes?" Moraga murmured, stopping just short of Griff's reach. The woman had clearly been around wulvers.

"Yes." Uldred shrugged his shoulder. "His eyes glowed red when he got angry."

"Ohhhh so I need t'tease the animal, then." Moraga chuckled. She turned and went to the corner of the tent, coming back with a long spear. Griff glanced into the corner, seeing his sword and belt were there. He watched her raise the spear, her eyes dancing with amusement. "Ye've been a vera bad doggie."

Griff growled at her, lips drawn back in a snarl.

"So can we use his blood?" Uldred asked, taking a seat on a cot at the other side of the tent as he watched his mother wielding her weapon, stalking toward the cage.

"Yer men did'na intercept t'wulvers?" Moraga sighed. "Raife an' t'rest of them rode in from t'coast—how'd ye manage t'miss 'em?"

"They followed them on the road," Uldred replied. "But then... they disappeared."

The woman snorted. "They did'na disappear into thin air!"

"No, but... mayhaps they found their way into the temple." Uldred glowered at Griff. "Mother, you said you could find it! You said your magic would be strong enough to open it!"

"Aye." She sighed, looking over at her son, soothing him. "All will be well. Ye've found six o'the lost packs a'ready! And they're all out there, followin' ye. They all b'lieve ye're t'red wulver of the prophecy, that ye're destined t'be t'Dragon King, the one who'll begin t'Blood Reign—"

"They only follow me because of your magic," he reminded her, pouting.

Griff stared between the two of them, stunned by this news. This Uldred had found *six* of the lost packs already? They were all camped out there, right now, following *him*? It was news that made Griff tremble with anger, and he worked hard to keep his eyes from flashing red with bloody rage.

"Aye. An' it will'na last fore'er!" she snapped. "I need t'wulver's blood!"

"Well we have his." Uldred pointed at Griff in the cage. "Isn't that good enough?"

"Mayhaps." She cocked her head, eyes narrowing at Griff as she took another step toward him. "He's a descendent. And they do say he's t'red wulver. Let's find out."

Moraga jabbed at Griff with the spear, moving quickly. Griff roared when the tip pierced his shoulder, blood pouring from the wound, and he grabbed the weapon, yanking it out of the woman's hands.

"Uldred!" Moraga cried for her son to rescue her as Griff pulled the spear and the witch along with it—she was still hanging on. It would be her undoing.

Griff howled, and outside, another wulver howled in response. Then another. And another. Uldred scowled, rushing toward the cage to save his mother from Griff, but it was too late.

Griff dropped the spear, circling the woman's throat with his big hand. He only needed one. He could snap her neck with a finger at this angle. She gasped, struggling as he lifted her feet off the floor, growling at Uldred.

"Get t'keys! Let me outta this cage!"

"Mother!" Uldred cried, taking a step back as Griff's other hand shot out to grab him.

Uldred just managed to sidestep.

Outside, the howling continued, and Uldred's face clouded with frustration and anger.

And, Griff noted, fear. He could smell it on the man.

"Uldred!" Moraga croaked, her long, red fingernails raking at Griff's hand, scratches that healed almost as fast as she made them. She was choking, her face turning blue.

"Help!" Uldred screamed. Literally screamed, something high pitched, like a woman. "Help! Help! Help!"

"Milord?" A wulver stuck his big head into the tent flap.

Griff howled, a sound that filled the tent, carrying far beyond, and the wulver at the door went wide-eyed at the sight. Then he threw back his head and howled too.

They're joining me. They know I'm the one. I'm their leader. They know...

Griff's brief moment of hope and the excitement that took flight in his chest was short-lived, as Moraga lifted her fist in front of her face. He actually laughed at the thought of this woman punching him, but something crunched between her fingers, something that sounded like bones and dry wings being powdered into dust.

The witch used her last bit of breath to blow the residue in his face.

It smelled like ancient death.

Griff coughed, suddenly, overwhelmingly nauseous.

Then everything went blurry, and he collapsed.

Bridget couldn't understand why Alaric hadn't come.

She hid high up in a tree, watching men and wulvers walking past, talking, laughing. She watched them set up tents and light fires. She watched, breath held, hand over her mouth to keep from crying out, as they untied Griff from the back of his horse, letting his big body slide, lifeless, to the ground.

She wouldn't believe he was dead, refused to believe it. They set up a cage and chained him into it, so she knew he still breathed. Bridget almost cried with relief. The tent went up around the cage, so she couldn't see him anymore. Two men guarded the front of the tent, but no one stood at the back. She could sneak underneath it, she decided. When it was full dark, when the camp slept.

So many wulvers, so many men! She'd never seen so many on little Skara Brae before.

But none of them were Alaric.

She left a clear trail for him to follow. He was an extraordinary tracker. If he'd come looking for her, he would have easily been able to follow. Why hadn't he come? He'd left to meet Raife and the other wulvers, who had come after Griff. And then…

And then…

She didn't want to think about it.

Bridget nearly fell asleep hugging the trunk of the tree, straddling a branch. She waited until the moon, still big and full, was high. She waited for most of the noise to die down. She waited until the man with the dirty-blonde hair and dark armor, the one she'd heard screaming, and the curvy blonde woman, left the tent, saying they were retiring for the night. The man gave orders to his men, told them to trade off a watch.

But there was still no one manning—or wulvering—the back of the tent.

Bridget had hoped her father would find them, but mayhaps he felt it too dangerous to approach with so many other wulvers and men around. She would have to rescue Griff herself, and take him back to the temple with her. She was grateful for the wulver ability to heal so quickly. If she could get him out of the cage—she had the pins in her hair, she might be able to pick the lock—he would be fine to travel.

The only thing she didn't see was Uri—Griff's horse. She would have liked to take him. And she hated the thought of leaving the animal there with the people—and wulvers—who treated Griff so badly. She didn't know who they were, or why they wanted Griff, but she knew they were bad news.

Bridget climbed slowly, carefully, down from the tree. She heard someone laugh and hid behind the tree, in the shadows, but there were no other voices. No one moved toward her or the tent. Peeking around the trunk, she saw just the two men—one man, one wulver—sitting on stools near the entrance. They were awake, watchful, talking softly, but not looking her way.

She moved as quietly as she could, sneaking around the back of the tent. Shimmying underneath it, she stopped as she cleared the material, finding herself inside the tent. There was no light to see by, but she heard him breathing. He was breathing. She knew he must be, but her heart fluttered at the reassurance. She just prayed there was no one else in the tent as she rolled to hands and knees and got her bearings.

"There's a lamp in t'corner, Bridget." Griff spoke in a hoarse whisper. "Front, on t'left."

Bridget startled, eyes wide when he spoke. But of course—he'd smelled her.

"Are ye a'righ'?" she whispered back, feeling her way in the dark. "Do I dare light t'lamp?"

"Keep it low."

She found the lamp, using the striker to light the oil lamp's wick. Then she quickly turned the flame low, not wanting anyone, especially the guards, to see it through the tent walls.

"Och, Bridget." Griff held his arms out to her and she went to him, finding herself trembling in his embrace through the cage bars.

"Yer hurt." She ran her hands over him, the wound in his shoulder. It was healing, but hadn't been healed entirely. "Who did this? Who are they?"

"We do'na have time fer questions." He kissed the top of her head, holding her closer, the bars digging into her flesh. She noticed they'd taken the muzzle off him at least, but his face was marked with long scratches. They were healing, too. "D'ye have t'key?"

She shook her head. "But we can break t'lock."

"Twill alert t'guards," Griff warned.

Tugging on the padlock, it held fast, but Bridget thought it wouldn't be difficult to break with a weapon. She had drawn her sword before he could stop her, bringing it down hard, cleaving the lock.

Griff was right—the human guard came in first, sword drawn, and Bridget whirled to meet him. Steel clashed and she winced. So much for staying quiet. The wulver guard ducked into the tent, already shifted in wulver-warrior form, growling, crossbow raised—and aimed directly at Bridget. Griff shoved his way out of the cage, the door hanging on its hinges as he busted through, the padlock in his hand. His chain caught him up short, but he managed to knock the other wulver aside and bring the heavy cage lock down onto the human guard's skull.

He groaned and dropped to the dirt.

Wulver faced wulver in the dim light, both growling low in their throats. Griff's eyes flashed red in the dark, making Bridget gasp in surprise, even as used to it as she'd grown. The other wulver hesitated. He'd seen it, too.

Bridget stared, stunned, as the other wulver sank slowly to one knee, bowing his head.

"My king," the other wulver growled. "How can I serve ye?"

Griff met her gaze, both of them so shocked it was hard to know exactly what to say or do.

"D'ye have t'keys?" Griff yanked on the chain attached to the collar around his neck.

"Aye." The other wulver rose, pulling out a set of keys and unlocking the collar. The guard looked between the two of them as he took a step back while Griff pulled off the collar and threw it to the floor.

"Thank ye," Griff said.

"Go, m'king," the other wulver said, keeping his voice low, reaching down and handing Griff his belt, sword and sheath. "Before they discover ye gone and raise t'alarm."

"I will'na forget this." Griff strapped on his belt, clapping the other wulver on the shoulder before grabbing Bridget's hand and ducking out of the tent. She followed him in the dark, both of them trying to be as quiet as they possibly could.

"Bridget," he whispered, pulling her behind the big tree she'd scaled and hid in. "M'father and 'is men came 'ere t'Skara Brae—are they at t'temple?"

"Alaric went ridin' out t'meet 'em," she told him, her brow knitting with worry. "We saw ye set upon by a band'o'men at t'same time. I said I'd follow ye, track ye, and leave a trail. But…"

Griff finished her sentence, "Alaric hasn't come after ye."

She shook her head, feeling tears stinging her eyes. Something must have happened, and from the look on Griff's face, he knew it, too.

"Listen, Bridget." He took her by the upper arms, talking low, close, looking into her face in the moonlight. "This man who took me, Uldred Lothienne—"

"Uldred Lothienne? *Lothienne*?" Her eyes widened. She knew the story of Eldred and Moraga—Griff had told her that story too. Had it been only last night that they were in each other's arms, talking and laughing? "Is it...? It can't be..."

"Aye, tis." His eyes flashed red in the dark. "Eldred and Moraga's son. He's mad—insane. He thinks he's t'red wulver—thinks he's t'one who'll bring together t'lost packs. These men—t'wulvers—they're all part of t'lost packs."

"But how..." Bridget had wondered at it, all of these wulvers out of their den, camped with an English leader, but now she knew, with a low, sinking feeling in her belly, not even waiting for Griff to answer. "Dark magic."

"Aye." Griff's eyes were blood red. "Moraga, his mother, is a witch. She's worked some magic on t'lost packs, but she needs m'blood—or m'father's—to enchant 'em further. T'compel 'em."

"Compel 'em t'do what?"

"T'go to war," Griff said flatly. "T'claim t'English throne from King Henry VIII. I imagine that's where Uldred'll start. Where 'is father left off."

"We hafta get back t'the temple." She swallowed, hoping, praying, that Alaric had met Raife and his men. That they were, even now, safe in the temple, thinking it too dangerous to travel with so many men and wulvers on the island.

But if they knew there were strange men and wulvers on the island—she couldn't imagine Alaric would let her stay out alone. Not this long. He would have come for her.

"Aye, but I need t'find Rory." Griff glanced around at the light of dying fires, tents set up all along the grass.

"Who?"

"Uldred has captured Rory MacFalon." Griff's voice was like steel. "More unfinished business, I imagine. Donal MacFalon killed Eldred Lothienne."

"Oh no..."

"We need t'find Rory and bring 'im to the temple. He's…" Griff sighed. "He's been tortured. Wulvers heal fast, and he looked… I can'na e'ven tell ye. Bad. Vera bad."

"Where would they keep 'im?" she whispered, knowing Rory was one of Griff's greatest friends.

"I do'na know." Griff looked around, swearing under his breath in at least two languages.

"We'll find 'im." Bridget took his hand, leading him this time in the darkness. "I was hidin' in this tree all day, watchin' them set up camp. I think I may know where he is…"

"Yer an angel," he breathed, stopping just for a moment to kiss her.

It was a hard, fast, breathless kiss and they were on their way again in an instant, but Bridget felt like she was flying. She was so relieved to have him with her, safe. No longer trapped, muzzled, chained in a cage.

"There's a tent near t'edge of their camp," she whispered as they crept closer to the rocky beach and the sea. "Isolated. I'd wager that's where they'd keep 'im…"

"Smart lass." Griff smiled at her when she looked back at him. The moon was still high, shining off the water, but the weather was changing, quickly. There was a low fog rolling in, hanging thick in the air.

"There." She pointed down at the beach, where a tent had been pitched, far away from anyone or anything else. She'd seen them setting it up from her vantage point in the tree and hadn't understood its purpose, but mayhaps now she knew.

"Ye stay 'ere," Griff whispered, wagging a finger at her.

"I do'na think so." She caught his finger in her hand, leaning in and gently biting the tip. "But I'll let ye go firs'…"

"Ye're impossible." He sighed, but cautioned her to be quiet as she followed him toward the tent.

There was very little cover out here in the open, but she was glad for the fog coming in. Besides, there seemed to be no one around. Except whoever was in the tent, of course. She hoped it would be lightly guarded, and they could free Rory and hurry back to the temple. Even without horses, they could make it back in under an hour.

Bridget stopped, hearing a low moan. She pulled on Griff's hand and he stopped, too. The walls of the tent were thin. Another moan, this one louder, carried toward them on the wind. Her belly clenched, wondering how badly hurt the wulver was. She hoped whatever horrible experiences he'd had were now at an end. The scrying pool had great healing properties. Even for wulvers.

She couldn't imagine how badly he had to have been tortured to be making the noises coming from the tent. Her eyes widened as she looked at Griff in the moonlight, and then saw his face change in an instant, the moment the sounds changed.

That wasn't a man moaning in pain, Bridget realized. It was a woman, moaning with pleasure. Bridget opened her mouth to say something, but Griff pulled her close, shaking his head and pressing his finger to his lips.

"Oh yes, yes, that's m'good boy, yesss!" A woman cried out, so loudly it made Bridget blush and she was glad for both the darkness and the fog, because she knew her face must match her hair. "Ohhh harder, harder!"

The feel of Griff's body against hers, arms encircling her waist, holding her close, made her want to melt against him. The sound of the two people making love in the tent brought thoughts and ideas into her head that she knew she shouldn't be thinking. But she was.

"Yes! Uldred! Yes! Ahhhhh!" The woman's voice rose to almost a scream, and Bridget realized now why the tent was pitched so far away from anyone else.

Obviously the wulver they were looking for wasn't here. Unless…

That's when the alarm was raised. The high sound of a horn in the distance, coming from the camp. Bridget would have gasped out loud if Griff hadn't put a hand over her mouth.

"Bloody hell!" They heard Uldred swear. "Mother, stay here. Don't move! I'll be right back."

Mother? Bridget's wide eyes met Griff's as he swept her back behind the tent, hand still covering her mouth. They stood there, right out in the open, hearing Uldred storming out of the tent and heading up the beach. He passed right by them in the darkness, swearing and stomping his boots over the rocks as he climbed the embankment toward camp.

She relaxed against Griff for just a moment, relieved they hadn't been discovered.

Bridget would have screamed out loud—did scream, behind the press of Griff's big hand over her mouth—when he dove toward the sand, taking them both down to the ground in an instant, covering her body with his. She didn't feel it for a moment. Above, the moon was big, but hazy, far away. Stars appeared between dark, low-hanging clouds like glittering jewels. She took all of that in, hearing the sound of the waves crashing against the shoreline, the distant shouts of men, and something humming, singing, close by. All of that registered before the pain.

"Are ye cut?" Griff rolled slightly off her—his weight was crushing her, in spite of the care he'd taken—hands roaming her body and she saw one of them come up bloody, almost black in the moonlight. "Och, Bridget, yer bleedin'!"

"Where?" But she knew. She felt the sting of it on her upper arm, and a sudden, queasy feeling, a dizziness that left her mouth dry and her hands trembling.

She didn't understand what had happened, not at first. But when she glanced over Griff's shoulder, she saw the ripped bit of tent flapping in the rising wind, a straight line right through the back of the canvas, about two feet long. That, alone, wouldn't have been enough to clue her in, but that humming sound drew her attention the other way, and she saw a big, half-moon blade sunk into an old, giant piece of driftwood on the embankment.

The blade was singing.

Enchanted.

She knew it immediately, and she knew something else too, as her blood flowed hot through her veins, the first wave of poison hitting her. Her heart skittered and jumped in her chest as she watched the blade try to pull itself from where it was buried in the driftwood. It gave an angry buzz, the hilt waving back and forth, like a fish trying to propel itself through the water.

The blade had been meant to kill her. And it was coming for her still. Bridget knew it, just as she knew the thing had been poisoned, and that poison was now in her bloodstream. Griff had saved her once again—she knew not how, because she hadn't heard anything, hadn't known the knife was coming—by throwing her to the ground.

"The blade's enchanted," she gasped, the pain in her arm finally, fully, hitting her. It burned, even as Griff put his hand over the wound, squeezing hard in an attempt to ebb the blood flow. "It'll keep comin' for me!"

"I'm more worried 'bout where't came *from*," he muttered, rolling again, taking them both to standing in an instant.

And of course, he was right to worry.

Bridget's reaction time was fast, but nowhere near as fast as his. Griff half-turned, keeping his hand on her upper arm, but still protecting her as much as he could with his own body as he drew his sword and the full force of the witch came at them from inside the tent.

She came through the tear in the fabric, like some sick, wrong thing birthing itself from the seam of hell, clawing her way through with long, red nails, her face appearing at the opening, sneering at them with a twisted snarl.

They weren't close enough for Griff to run her through—he'd initially rolled them far enough away from the tent in order to make their escape—but the witch saw his sword, his ready stance, and hesitated. Her gaze skipped from them to the blade that jerked and thrashed, trying to pry itself free from the piece of wood.

"She's callin' t'blade," Bridget whispered to Griff, hearing the woman speaking words low in her throat. "Tis enchanted!"

"There's n'such thing," he snapped, glancing at the witch, whose attempts at widening the tear in the fabric were increasing, and then down at Bridget. "I hafta get ye to safety, lass. We hafta stop yer bleedin'..."

"Aye..." She wasn't going to disagree. She didn't know if it was the poison she was sure had been on the blade, or the fact that she was losing so much lifeblood, but either way, she was growing faint. "Hurry..."

Griff was torn, she saw it on his face. He wanted to finish the witch, here and now, but he also needed to take Bridget to safety. He gave a low growl, lunging forward as the witch pushed her head through the opening, her chants louder, and Bridget saw the knife, the blade still dripping with Bridget's blood, had pulled another two inches out of the wood. It was nearly free. And when it was free, it would come for her again.

Griff brought his sword up one-handed, raising it high with a low growl, and then brought it down at the witch's neck. If it had been as fast and sharp as a scythe blade, it would have severed her head from her neck instantly. But the witch sensed it coming and pulled back, like a turtle into its shell.

"We need t'blade," Bridget murmured, feeling herself slipping toward blackness, fighting it, hard.

"Bridget..." Griff frowned, looking between her and the knife.

"Trust me, Griff, please," she pleaded. "We need that blade...."

He gave a frustrated growl, but he turned and brought his sword down at the knife. That just snapped the hilt, breaking it off, and they both heard a low cry come from inside the tent, as if the witch and the knife were one. But at least the blade stopped moving, stopped that incessant buzzing sound as it tried to free itself and fly again. The magic in it had been broken.

Griff swung his sword again, knocking the full curve of the blade free, and Bridget grabbed it before he could, using the edge of her plaid. Griff's head came up and Bridget heard it too. The sound of mounted men approaching, coming from the encampment.

"Hurry," she whispered, turning to hide her face against his chest as he lifted her in his arms, carrying her quickly away from the tent, heading down the rocky beach. The blade rested in her lap, its curved edge glinting in the moonlight. Looking back, she saw the men on the embankment, saw their horses heading down it toward the tent where they had just been. She saw the witch, too, her face appearing at the front of the tent flap as Griff made his way toward the shoreline, saw the blonde's lips moving, chanting, mayhaps still talking to her blade, but it sang no more.

"Where're we goin'?" Bridget leaned her head back against Griff's shoulder, thinking, *There's nowhere to go.* They were trapped, with a hundred armed horsemen and a witch at their back, and nothing but the endless sea in front of them.

Griff slid her into a boat, pushing it into the water as he did. He hopped in, already rowing, as Bridget struggled to sit up, looking behind them as the horseman reached the beach. There were boats, she saw, lining the shore, tied up together, attached to the ship with the dragon's head on the prow anchored further out. Uldred's ship, the one he'd clearly brought them all in on.

"Stem that bleedin'," Griff growled, pulling harder on the oars. "Hurry!"

Bridget winced, not wanting to look at her wound, but she grabbed the edge of her plaid, setting the blade aside, seeing its wicked edge still stained with her blood, and tore the edge of the material. She wrapped her upper arm tight, as best she could, tying it using her mouth on one end of the strip and her hand on the other.

"I can'na outrow 'em, lass..." Griff pulled hard on the oars, his big muscles working, but Bridget saw the men in boats, some with four, five, six of them oaring in one vessel. That much manpower would win out, even over one wulver.

"I'll help ye." She grabbed a set of oars, wincing at the pain in her arm, but she knew it was useless. As she rowed, bright red blood bloomed, darkening the plaid wrapped around her upper arm. Bridget saw Griff's wound now, a matching gash on his upper arm. It had broken open with his effort and was bleeding again.

"Griff, wait." Bridget glanced back, seeing two of the boats had gained much ground. They were only a boat-length away, maybe two, and gaining, although due to the fog coming in, she couldn't see the shore anymore. "Give me yer hands."

"I need t'row wit' m'hands!" he snapped.

"Trust me!" she urged, pulling her oars into the boat and reaching for him.

"More magic?" Griff glanced at the gaining rowboats, and then at her. He sighed, pulling the oars in, his big hands swallowing hers as he clasped them.

Bridget took a deep breath, closed her eyes, and began to incant the words she hoped, prayed, would work.

"I hope yer magic can make us disappear," he grumbled, distracting her. "They're still gainin' on us..."

"Shhh!" Bridget cocked an eye open. "Concentrate with me..."

"What am I concentratin' on?"

"Us." She squeezed his hands in hers. "Concentrate on us, Griff..."

When she said that, she instantly felt the energy shift. The tides rocking the boat shifted underneath them. And when Bridget opened her eyes a moment later, she saw the fog that had been slowly gathering had thickened. She could barely see Griff, just a foot from her in the boat. And they had a tail wind, pushing them further out to sea.

"Did ye do that?" Griff frowned, his hands tightening over hers.

"We did that." She gave a relieved sigh. She could hear the men in the boats calling to one another. They sounded far away, but that could have been a trick of the fog. "But you'd better keep rowin'..."

"Aye." He let go of her hands, grabbing the oars again.

In the rush of trying to escape, Bridget hadn't had a moment to think, but now that they were floating out on the water, sailing away from an island she'd never left in her life, it hit her. Alaric and Aleesa were on that island, and she had no idea if they were safe. Griff's father, Raife, and his men were there, too. And his friend, Rory MacFalon. They would have to go back, they would have to make their way to the temple, find a way to...

Bridget remembered the blade and realized her wound had stopped aching. It had gone numb.

The poison.

"Griff..." Her heart lurched in her chest when she realized what Moraga had done. But she had to be sure.

"What is't, lass?" Griff pulled hard on the oars, his breath coming in short pants. He was rowing as fast as he could. The fog was so thick, there was no way to tell which way they were going—but given the wind she'd called up, she hoped it was due south.

Bridget found the blade, holding it up in the darkness. There was little light there in the fog. It even dampened the bright light of the moon from above. But she didn't need to see it to know. She just needed to taste.

Bridget brought the tip of the blade to the end of her tongue. There was blood, coppery and bitter. The metallic taste of the blade itself. And a tinny sort of heat, something that burned the tip of her tongue before she spit it out.

Griff had stopped rowing, watching her with interest.

"What is't?" he asked again, this time his voice sounding much softer, concerned.

"Poison." Even as she said it, she felt it. She'd suspected it when the blade had cut her, but now she knew for sure. Aleesa had trained her in the ways of dark magic—not so she could ever use it, but so that she knew how to recognize it. And combat it, if need be. There were those who would come to the Temple of Asher and Ardis for healing, and much of that healing had to do with undoing the black magic attempted by others.

"Poison?" Griff's voice was barely a whisper. She'd never heard him scared before, but there was a hint of fear in his voice. "What can be done?"

"T'Witch's Kiss," she said bitterly. "Tis poison an' curse. If't penetrates, deep into t'body, it'll kill quickly, almos' instantly."

"But t'blade jus' scratched us."

Well, it had just scratched him, Bridget realized. Her wound was deeper. And, she wasn't a wulver, with the ability to heal herself so quickly. The poison would work faster in her.

"Aye," she agreed, trying to remember everything Aleesa had taught her about this particular poison and curse. "If it does'na penetrate righ' away, it'll kill slowly. Painfully."

"How slowly?"

"A week." She swallowed. She didn't know if it was real or her imagination, but she was beginning to feel faint. "Mayhaps a lil more'o'less..."

"Can Aleesa heal ye?" Griff reached for her and Bridget went to him, letting him fold her into his arms. His heart was beating hard and fast in his chest and she pressed her ear against the steady sound. "Bridget! Can Aleesa undo this?"

"Nay..." she whispered, shaking her head. There were some things she could do—pack the wound with seaweed, mayhaps, when they got to shore, to draw some of the poison. But it wouldn't stop the progression. She told him this as she trembled against him. She could almost feel the witch's poison working its way through her blood.

"Bridget!" Griff lifted her face so he could search her eyes. His were blood red, blazing. "There has t'be somethin' to stop't! Wha' can I do?"

The witch had chosen her weapon well, Bridget realized, finally remembering what Aleesa had told her about this particular poison, and its only remedy.

"The Isle of the Dragon." She sighed. It might as well have been the moon. They were in a rowboat. Even with a wulver rowing, they wouldn't reach it in time unless Griff could fly. "There's a temple on t'Isle of the Dragon. It's northwest of t'Isle of Man."

"The Isle of the Dragon?" Griff blinked in surprise. "'Tis where t'largest of t'lost packs is supposed to be—accordin' to what Aleesa gave me..."

"Hmm..." She smiled, feeling her eyes beginning to close. She was so very tired. "But there's no such thing as fate..."

"If there is, then yer mine, lass." Griff pressed his lips to her forehead, holding her so close it was hard to breathe. Or mayhaps that, too, was the poison working its way through her. "If I b'lieved in true mates, ye'd be mine..."

"Ye do'na need t'b'lieve..." She felt his lips meet hers under the cover of the fog, and she kissed him back, using the last of her energy to wrap her arms around his thick neck and cling to him.

She whispered the truth against his mouth as they parted, "I a'ready know..."

And then she let the fog roll in and claim her completely.

⚜

When she woke in Griff's arms, she thought she'd died and gone to heaven.

They rocked together in softness. There was no pain— well, only a little, when she moved her arm. She noticed it when she lifted her hand to touch his stubbly cheek in the morning light. Mayhaps they'd both died and gone to heaven, she thought, seeing the way his thick, sooty lashes touched his cheeks. But the big wulver lying beside her was breathing, soft and shallow. He was on guard, even in his sleep, she realized, tracing the line of his mouth, suddenly longing for the press of his lips.

When she lifted her gaze, she saw his eyes were open. They were clear, gold, and looking at her with so much concern it broke her heart. She took in her surroundings in an instant, realizing their slow rocking was the motion of a boat. Nay, a ship. They were in a small state room, and she could see the sun shining on the water through a porthole.

"Tis good t'see yer eyes, lass." His voice was hoarse. "They've been closed fer two days."

Two days gone. Two days wasted.

She glanced at her wound, seeing it had been rebandaged. Looking closer, she blinked at him in surprise.

"Did ye pack it wit' seaweed?" she asked.

"Jus' like ye tol' me." He smiled.

A knock sounded on the door. "Bryce!"

"Bryce?" She giggled. "Who's Bryce?"

"I'm Bryce and yer Busby." Griff grinned. "Oh an'— yer a boy."

"A boy?" she squeaked, suddenly offended. "I'm not a—"

"Shh!" He pulled the covers up to her neck, gathering her hair in a knot at the back of her head. He took another frowning look, rolling her hip so she was pointing sideways. "Hide those damnable curves!"

She giggled at that, pulling the covers up so only her eyes appeared.

"Aye?" Griff pulled the door open.

"More seaweed fer t'lad," the voice said. It was low and gruff.

"Thank ye, MacMoran," Griff said.

"How's he doin'?" the voice asked.

"A lil better. He woke up a few moments ago," Griff replied. "We'll need some food."

"Aye, I'll bring ye some."

"Thank ye," Griff called, closing the door again.

"Where're we?" Bridget sat, looking down and seeing that, aside from the bandage on her arm, she was wearing nothing at all.

Griff noticed, too. His eyes moved over her body before she pulled the sheet back up to her chin.

"T'Sea Wolf," he said, putting the seaweed pack aside on the bureau.

"Is that a ship?" she asked.

"Aye." Griff's hand fell to her hip, over the covers, tracing her curves through it. "Uldred would've expected us t'follow the coast southeast t'Wick... so I rowed southwest to Thurso an' that's where I found Cap'n Blackburn. He was headin' to the Isle of Man."

Her eyes widened. "Wit' what cargo?"

"Do'na ask." Griff chuckled. "Ye do'na wanna know."

"Tis a pirate ship," she whispered, his look confirming her suspicions.

"Aye." He nodded gravely. "That's why I disguised ye as a lad."

"I've really been out fer two whole days?" she lamented, capturing his hand in hers and lacing their fingers. She brought his hand to her mouth, kissing his knuckles. She didn't like to think of him being alone, worried about her, that whole time. She licked one of his fingers, meeting his glowing gaze. Then she sucked his fingertip into her mouth.

"Two and a half, aye," he agreed, groaning as he watched her. "But yer awake now."

"I jus' hafta keep pretendin' t'be a boy." She was rather offended by this predicament, spitting his finger out and half-sitting. She struggled, though. Her arm burned. She winced, knowing they'd have to keep the bandages changed.

If they could make it to the island, if they could get the antidote...

"T'was t'bes' way t'keep ye safe on this ship," Griff said, helping steady her with a hand at her elbow as she sat. "Pirates aren't known fer their morals, lass."

"Neither are wulvers." She felt dizzy, just sitting up, but she put her arms around his neck anyway, pressing herself fully against him. She heard him moan a little through their kiss, and she found, when she let her hand wander under his plaid, just how much he'd missed her while she was passed out.

"Besides, this way, we get t'share a cabin," he murmured, nuzzling her hair. "Och, yer hair, m'love... I shoulda cut it, but I could'na bear to..."

"What'd ye promise 'em t'get 'em t'take ye t'the Isle o't'Dragon?" she wondered aloud, squeezing his shaft, making him shift and groan. "Mos' men think tis haunted"

"M'firs' born," he said, laughing when she jerked back to stare at him. "I'm kiddin', lass. I would ne'er promise our bairns to anyone..."

"Our bairns." Tears stung Bridget's eyes. The thought of having children with this man delighted her. And at the same time, she knew, could feel the poison coursing through her blood. Mayhaps it would never happen, after all.

"Shh, m'love," he whispered, stroking her hair. She rested her cheek on his chest, and then saw it—a thick, dark line along his bicep. Frowning she traced it with her finger. "What's this? Griff? Were ye cut too? Wit' the witch's knife?"

"Aye." He looked down at it. "Tis numb. I do'na think the poison got into me."

"Och, you insufferable wulver!" Bridget grabbed for the seaweed. "It's in yer blood, trust me! It may take longer, but it'll kill ye, just like it's gonna kill me!"

"It's not gonna kill ye." Griff grabbed her by the shoulders. Her wound ached when he did that, and he saw the pain on her face and let go a little. "We're goin' t'the isle—we'll find this mage. And he's goin t'cure ye. And then we'll get back in time for t'eclipse, like Alaric said we had to, before… whatever magical thing happens then. And I'll kill Uldred and that witch meself wit' m'bare hands."

"Before t'eclipse?" Bridget raised her eyebrows in surprise. Alaric had told Griff to come back before the eclipse? But why? "Did Alaric tell ye? That's when I'm supposed t'take m'vows as a priestess. Although now…"

She swallowed, looking down at her burning wound—there was something dark seeping through the bandage.

"We a'ready threw that plan out t'window." Griff smiled. "Yer mine, Bridget. I told ye I'd come back fer ya…"

"Instead, I came t'find ye…" She smiled. Then she looked at her wound, lamenting the way things had gone. "If we'd just gone straight t'the beach. If only that stupid knife hadn't…"

"Listen!" He shook her again. "We're gonna find a cure fer this. I do'na care, whate'er it is, whate'er works! Ye hear me, Bridgit? I will'na lose ye."

"Aye." A little smile played on her lips. "I hear ye. D'ye hear yerself?"

Griff stopped, then gave a little, sheepish smile. "T'isn't necessarily magic. Mayhaps it's some herbal cure. M'own mother knows herbs, and she—"

"B'lieve what ye want." Bridget pressed the seaweed against his upper arm. "But tis magic."

"No more than that is." Griff reached for a clean bandage, letting her tie it around his upper arm.

"It's all magic, ye silly wulver." Bridget slowly climbed into his lap.

She was still dizzy, feeling feverish, but she didn't care. She prayed that her mother had been right—that there was a mage named Raghnall on the Isle of the Dragon, and that he had some sort of antidote, or could at least concoct one, for the Witch's Kiss. She could do nothing but hope, as the poison made its way through her body, and trust, that what should be, would be.

In the meantime, she was going to make love to this man. While she was conscious, as long as she was breathing, she wanted him inside her and nowhere else. Griff kissed her back, his hands roaming over her hot, feverish flesh, and she felt how much he wanted her through his plaid and longed to feel him, skin to skin.

A knock on the door interrupted them again.

Griff groaned, shaking his head in denial.

"I'm starvin'!" she confessed, nibbling on his ear.

"Well, that mus' be a good sign." He slid her reluctantly off his lap.

"I'm goin' to eat e'erythin'," she told him, sliding the sheet ever so slowly up her thighs. She watched his gaze follow it. "Then Busby's gonna come back to bed and show Bryce the whole world."

Bridget parted her thighs and Griff gave a low growl, grabbing her knees and shoving his face between them. She had to bite her own lip to keep from screaming as he devoured her, front to back, up and down, like a starving man.

The knock came again, insistent.

"Ye better get that," she gasped as he lifted his face, covered with her juices, and wiped it with the back of his hand.

"A'righ', lass," he croaked. "I'll let ye eat somethin'— but then I'm gonna eat ye!"

Bridget pulled the covers up again, all the way up, as Griff went to get the door.

No matter what happened, they were going to make the most out of whatever time they had left.

Chapter Nine

Griff held a sleeping Bridget against him as he rode his borrowed horse the last half mile or so. She was weakening day by day, and he couldn't bear to watch it.

He'd never wanted to believe in magic more than when he stood at the door of the temple on the Isle of the Dragon, calling out, seeking entrance. He hoped there wasn't a guardian—someone he would have to fight—although considering the mood he was in, letting off a little steam chopping of someone's limbs wasn't exactly a bad idea.

He just didn't want to have to waste the time.

"Please! We seek entrance! She needs healin'!" Griff boomed, his voice carrying over the rolling, green hills of the island—and, he hoped, deep into the temple, where a healer waited.

The island itself was bigger than Skara Brae—it had only taken him twenty minutes to ride into the island, using Bridget's instructions to find the temple. At least this one wasn't hidden. He'd seen it a mile away, marked by an open-air stone circle out front that towered up toward the sky. The temple itself had tall, Greek-style columns and a giant door, but it was all in serious disrepair. The door was twice the size of Griff himself.

The door opened and an old man peered out through the smallest of cracks. Bridget had prepared him for this mage—a man, Aleesa had told her daughter, who was said to be a direct descendent of Merlin himself. He was the head of all of the temples of Asher and Ardis located around Scotland, England, Ireland and Wales, but as the wulvers had begun to be hunted and die out, the old man had become reclusive. Bridget said her mother and father had met him only once and that no one had seen him in over twenty years.

Griff was about to change that.

"You!" The heavy door creaked open a little further, revealing a face lined with age, a thick, bushy white beard, which was odd, considering the old man had almost no hair on his head at all. "Both of you! Oh this won't do at all. What are you doing here? You can't be here!"

The old man turned, mumbling to himself, leaving the door slightly ajar. Griff blinked, staring after him.

"Well come on then!" the old man called. "And mind you close and lock the door behind you!"

Griff was too surprised to do anything else. He pushed the door open and closed it behind him, stooping to turn the lock. In his arms, Bridget stirred. He leaned in, pressing his lips to her throat, taking her pulse and temperature at once. She was still warm. And her pulse was far too fast. She'd told him this would happen, the closer the poison got to her heart.

"Come, come, come!" The old man shuffled through the temple and Griff followed. They rounded a circle, marked by more Greek columns, and he saw an arena down below, lined with hundreds of seats. What happened down there? Griff wondered, as the old man took a turn and pushed his way through another door.

"She's been poisoned," Griff told the old man as they entered a room so filled with artifacts, scrolls, and books, Griff literally had to shuffle through them on the floor. "We need yer help."

"You can't be here." The old man sighed, pointing upward, and Griff looked, surprised to find a model of the solar system spinning above their heads. Griff had seen them in books his mother shared with him when he was a small boy, except in those books, all of the planets and the sun had moved around the little blue marble called Earth. In this model, the sun was its center.

"I need yer help, old man," Griff snapped, clearing off a table of books and scrolls and putting Bridget on it. "She's been poisoned and we need the antidote. I know ye have it!"

"You both need to be here, and soon!" The old man pointed at the model, shaking his nearly-bald head. "On Skara Brae. Not here, in my temple! You need to be there for the solar eclipse. You're entirely too far south—and west! The Dragon and the Lady will be there, not here. Oh, well, they will be here, too, because they are everywhere, but they won't be here, if you take my meaning. This won't do at all!"

Griff sighed in frustration. The old man was babbling in some strange accent—it was hard to place. Definitely not Scottish, but not exactly English either.

"Raghnall!" Griff called the old man's name—Bridget had shared it with him—and he startled, looking at him over a pair of rimless spectacles.

"Griff?" Bridget spoke his name, faint, from where he'd placed her on the wooden table. "Did ye say... are we here?"

She struggled to sit and he helped her. The old man frowned between the two of them, shaking his bald head.

"I'm a servant of t'sun an' t'moon." Bridget's voice was low, almost too soft to be heard, as she spoke to Raghnall. "I await t'blade an' chalice."

"Yes, yes, I know who you are! Both of you." Raghnall waved her formality away, lifting his nose and sniffing the air. He frowned, taking a step closer to Bridget, reaching out to lift the bandage on her arm. Griff didn't like to look at it. It had gone black, ugly, thick threads of darkness reaching up toward her shoulder, across her collarbone, toward her heart. "The Witch's Kiss! You're going to die soon! Oh, that won't do at all! Why didn't you say something, son?"

"I tol' ye before y'even answered t'door!" Griff roared, holding onto Bridget as she leaned against him, eyes closing once more. She was barely hanging on.

"Wise and skilled use of this Seatwist poultice," the old man mused, studying the wound. "It's saved your life, but it won't keep the Witch's Kiss from reaching your heart."

"That's why we're 'ere." Griff managed this through gritted teeth. He also managed to keep from putting the old man, head first, into his enormous shelves of books, but only because he hadn't yet produced the antidote they needed. "She's dyin', and as ye say, *that can'na happen.* She told me t'bring 'er 'ere because ye've a cure fer this dark magic!"

"I do?" Raghnall looked at Griff, tilting his head in surprise. Then his face brightened. "Oh, yes, you know, I probably do! Come!"

Griff groaned in frustration as the old man pushed his way through yet another door. Griff picked Bridget up again, carrying her through the entryway, following the little man into another room, this one more laboratory than library. There were hundreds of bottles lining the shelves on the walls, all various colors and sizes. Griff looked for a place to set Bridget down, seeing a long table in the corner, but it was occupied. A red blanket covered what had to be a giant body underneath, at least twelve feet tall. As he watched, Griff thought he saw one end of the blanket flutter. The end near the head.

Griff found a chair instead, knocking several books to the floor, and sat in it, Bridget tucked into his lap, as the old man assembled things on a table in front of him. The little man hummed to himself as he worked while Griff watched, impatient. Bridget stirred again in his arms and he looked down at her. She opened her eyes, smiling up at him, dazed, but still there. Still his Bridget. She looked over at the table where Raghnall worked, watching.

"Could he move any slower?" Griff complained.

"Shhh." Bridget shook her head. "Let t'man work."

Raghnall made an owl sound and, out of seemingly nowhere, an owl swooped down from a higher shelf, landing beside Raghnall on the table. The old man leaned in to whisper something into the bird's ear, an action so ridiculous, Griff laughed out loud.

"You have to speak quietly to owls," the old man explained. "Their ears are very sensitive, you know."

Griff looked at Bridget and she shrugged, smiling. "Tis true."

"I'm goin' mad." Griff snorted, blinking as the old man made a rasping noise on the table and the biggest, blackest snake Griff had ever seen slithered out from underneath. His hand went for his sword, but Bridget stopped him.

"Don't ye dare!" she gasped. She had no strength left in her limbs, but her tone stopped him anyway.

The snake, its eyes almost as gold as Griff's, started making its way up one of the shelves behind the old man, while the owl, who had a bottle clutched in its talons, dropped it in front of him. Griff thought it would shatter and spill its contents everywhere, but Raghnall's reflexes were eerily fast, and he caught it in one hand without even looking up from the book he was consulting. Then the snake had returned, too, a box twisted in its coils that it deposited on the table for the old man.

"Could ye hurry't up?" Griff called as Bridget's head drooped again. He could see her bandaged arm, a thick, dark liquid beginning to seep from underneath. The smell of it was nauseating. Then he glanced at his own arm. His wound was still there—astounding, given his wulver healing abilities. It was a thick, dark line under his skin. He'd been poisoned too, but the effects were taking longer. He might have another week beyond Bridget. Not that it mattered. If she died, he would die too. He couldn't live without this woman, he knew that now.

The old man ignored Griff's protest and pleas to move faster. He mixed and hummed, hummed and mixed. The owl flew back up to its perch, tucking its head under a wing. The snake slithered back under the table, where Griff could see nothing but one yellow eye. Raghnall went to the fireplace to fetch a teapot.

"D'ye have t'blade that cut ye?" Raghnall glanced up at Griff, looking at him over his glasses.

"Oh, aye." Griff reached into the pack over his shoulder, drawing out the curved, half-moon blade, now missing its hilt.

"Moraga." Raghnall shook his bald head, taking the blade from Griff's hands. "You're both lucky to be alive, son."

"Aye." Griff knew it was true. The witch had nearly killed them both. If he hadn't heard, a split second before the knife had ripped through the tent fabric, the witch's whispered incantation, it would have found its way through both of them, right into their hearts. They would have died together there on that beach. And, he'd thought, several times on this insane trip toward the Isle of the Dragon, that mayhaps that would have been preferable to watching Bridget fade slowly away from him. He couldn't bear to see her in pain—and knowing he had to do this, to save her, while his kin's fate on Skara Brae was completely unknown to him, was anathema. For a man whose patience was thin, it was pure torture.

The only comfort was, if this worked, if Raghnall could do what Bridget claimed, the largest of the lost packs was here on the Isle of the Dragon. Somewhere. He just had to find them.

"Come along!" Raghnall called, glancing over his shoulder at Griff as he went out the door once again. "Oh, and bring the teapot!"

"We do'na have time fer tea, ol' man," Griff growled, rising, with Bridget in his arms.

But he picked up the teapot and carried it anyway, following the old man down the hall, around the circle, into another room.

This place, he recognized. It was like the spring in his den at home. Or the scrying pool on Skara Brae. Except this room was far bigger, and definitely more architectually complex.

"Come, come!" Raghnall waved him over. He took the teapot from Griff—it was quite hot—and put it aside on a rock. He had the knife on another, flat rock. The old man gathered water from the pool in his cupped hands, letting it fall over the blade.

Griff stared as the knife hissed, making a high-pitched noise, almost as if it were crying. Then it began to melt. It turned into a liquid metal, like quicksilver, that glistened and pooled in droplets on the rock's surface.

"Excellent." The old man nodded, producing a spoon from somewhere in his robe, scooping up some of the liquid and putting it into the teapot. Bandages appeared from somewhere in the old man's robes, too, and he poured some of the liquid from the teapot onto them. Then he poured the liquid into a clay chalice.

"Bring her here." Raghnall pointed to a large, flat rock, about waist-high.

Griff carried Bridget over to it, stretching her out on the rock. The hair he'd carefully hidden and tied back, tucking it under her cap before they left the ship so no one would know she was a woman, had come undone and spilled over the dark slab like fire. Her eyes remained closed, her face flushed with fever. He pulled her tunic down on one shoulder, revealing her wound, the fabric stained with darkness. Blood and pus and God only knew what else. Dark magic.

But I don't believe in magic.

He wasn't so sure anymore, as he watched the old man remove Bridget's dressing, tossing the pungent bandage aside. He applied the new bandage. It was thin, wet, hardly enough to soak up the awful liquid seeping from her arm, and Griff frowned at it, doubting as the old man plastered it over the wound. It stuck, as if magic, adhering to the gash.

"That'll do." Raghnall nodded, eyes narrowed, watching.

Griff watched, too, seeing the dark lines on her skin, the ones stretching like tree branches stretching toward her heart, starting to fade before his very eyes.

"It worked," Griff breathed, the relief flooding his chest so palpable it felt as if someone had just lifted the weight of his horse from it. "Oh thank God, tis workin'!"

"Of course it is." The old man rolled his eyes, shaking his head. Then, he turned to Griff and slapped one of the bandages on his upper arm, where the dark line appeared. That spot on his skin had gone oddly numb to the touch, and a few times, he'd felt strange, lightheaded, but other than that, he'd been uneffected. Not like Bridget.

"That should do for you, wulver." Raghnall winked. "The Witch's Kiss would have taken another month to kill you, I'd wager. Your species is quite strong."

Griff shrugged. He didn't care about his wound. All he cared about was that Bridget was opening her eyes. And this wasn't the sort of half-awake state of being she'd been in for the past day or so. Her gaze was clear, eyes bright, with that delightful, grey-green sparkle he had come to seek whenever they were in the same room.

"Now, drink." Raghnall lifted the chalice to Bridget's lips as she sat up on the rock. Griff gave her a hand—she was still acting slightly tipsy, but oh, so much better than before. Coming back, instead of fading away. He could tell already.

Bridget drank readily, gulping down the hot liquid. Griff, on the other hand, turned his nose up when she offered it to him.

"Yer not invincible, wulver," she snapped, and Griff had to grin at her tone. Oh yes, Bridget was back. "Now drink!"

Griff crinkled his nose in protest—the stuff smelled almost as bad as the bandage that had come off Bridget's arm—but he drank it anyway. It made him gag.

"Such a lil bairn." Bridget teased when he handed the now empty cup to Raghnall.

"That's awful." Griff shuddered.

"The bandage will dissolve over time." Raghnall made sure Bridget's was still affixed. It was like a second skin. "It will keep working until then against the poison."

"That's it?" Griff snorted, blinking as he looked between the two of them. "We sail all the way here for a new bandage and a tea party?"

Raghnall snickered. "Oh, I forgot to mention—you have to go outside and do a rain dance. Like the Mongols. Mayhaps you'd like to sacrifice a virgin? Or at least scare one, like the Norsemen?"

Bridget giggled, a sound that made Griff's heart soar. She poked Griff in the shoulder—his uninjured one.

"Don't mind 'im," she said, still laughing. "He does'na trust magic... yet."

"Doesn't trust magic?" Raghnall huffed. "That's like not believing you'll get wet if you piss into the bloody wind!"

Griff snorted and rolled his eyes but he didn't protest.

Mostly because Bridget was laughing, more bright-eyed and aware than she'd been in days. And the feeling had suddenly come back into his arm, where he could see that thick, dark line had begun to fade.

"Thank ye fer yer help," Griff said to the old man. He'd been ready to put him through a wall when they first arrived, but now he just wanted to kiss him. Or, at least hug him. "Can ye tell me... there's a lost wulver pack on this isle. D'ye know where tis?"

The man looked up from where he was gathering his things. Then he grinned, and Griff noted it was more toothless than not.

"Lost pack?" The old man chuckled. Then he laughed out loud. "Lost pack? Oh that's rich!"

Griff and Bridget exchanged confused glances. But Griff was getting used to being confused around the old man.

"Aye, a lost pack of wulvers," Griff explained slowly. "A den. They'd 'ave a den 'ere, somewhere on t'isle."

"There's no lost pack, son." Raghnall smiled, picking up his teapot. "They know exactly where they are, and if they want you to find them, they'll let you know. You being who you are, I'm sure they'll find you, soon enough."

Griff spread his fingers helplessly at Bridget. "This man talks in circles."

"The world moves in circles." The old man snorted, rotating his finger in the air near his temple. "Now, you two need to rest. That brew hasn't really hit you yet, and when it does, you'd both best be lying down."

"We need t'get back t'the ship." Griff frowned, but Bridget was up—she was up and walking, following the old man!—and so he went after them.

"In here." The old man nodded to a mattress. It looked big and soft compared to the one on the ship.

And suddenly, Griff was tired. Beyond. Exhausted.

"Come." Bridget pulled him toward the bed.

"You two will be fine in here." The old man gave a nod. "I'll rustle up some food for later."

"But..." Griff protested as Bridget pushed him onto the mattress. She was already pulling off his boots.

Raghnall licked his finger, holding it up, as if testing an invisible wind. "If we leave tomorrow, by noon, we'll get back in time."

"We? What?" Griff shook his head, confused, and the world tilted. Everything came unhinged. "What the hell?"

"Shhh." Bridget thanked Raghnall—he heard that much—before shutting the door and coming back to the bed.

The last thing he saw was her slipping out of her plaid and sliding into bed with him. Her body was warm—but not as warm as it had been—as she stretched out on top of him, pulling the covers over. He felt the urge to take her, felt his cock rising between her thighs, but something else was taking over his body. The blood in his veins felt thick with it, a hot pulse that made everything hazy, blurry. It was like being drunk—only far, far worse.

"Bridget," he whispered against her lips, so soft and plump. She was smiling.

"Shhhh," she urged, tucking her head under his chin, resting her cheek on his chest. "Sleep."

And he did.

When he woke, Bridget was gone. At first, he didn't know where he was, but then he saw a clean plaid and tunic beside him on the bureau. His sword was still there. He dressed quickly, sheathing his sword, and headed out to look for her.

He couldn't believe how good he felt. For days, since his altercation with Uldred on Skara Brae, he'd been worried sick about Bridget, and when he wasn't caring for and fretting over her, he'd been consumed with thoughts of his pack. He'd been so concerned with other things, he hadn't noticed his own declining health. He was a wulver, so he was from hearty stock. Even big wounds often wouldn't kill a wulver. His uncle, Darrow, had once been run through with a long sword and survived.

But the poison had clearly affected him more than he realized. The world looked brighter, clearer, as he stepped into the temple hallway and glanced around. The open-air stadium below was quiet. But he heard talking to his right. Bridget's laugh. The sound made him smile and he headed toward it.

"Yes, that's just right," Raghnall said, smiling over his cluttered table at Bridget. "You'd make a fine priestess."

"She'll make a fine wife," Griff growled, shuffling through the books and papers on the floor to put an arm around her from behind.

Bridget smiled back at him, and he couldn't believe the transformation in her. She was dressed like a queen, in a white and silver robe, with silver combs in her thick, red hair. It tumbled down her shoulders, washed and brushed, shining like fire in the light that came in from the high windows above. It made him want to take her straight back to bed. But he knew better. There was an incredible urgency in him, flowing through his blood, now that he was awake. More fully awake than he'd been in days, to be sure.

"Guardian, priestess, wife, mother, she is all of those things." Raghnall nodded. "Now that you're awake, warrior, it's time for us to break bread and be on our way."

"Our?" Griff frowned at the old mage. "You're coming with us?"

"Of course." The mage laughed. "Why do you think destiny sent you here, young prince who would be king?"

"Destiny again." Griff snorted, and when he did, he caught a whiff of roast meat. His stomach growled. "Destiny and prophecy and magic. You can counteract some witch's cursed blade but you can't tell me where the lost packs are on the isle?"

"They've already found you." Raghnall chuckled and Griff bristled in response.

"Where?" He glanced around, as if a pack of wulvers might be coming through the door.

"As Dragon King, you'll have to learn to read the energy of magic," the old man informed him. "You'll have to trust it. Like you read the weather. Or like learning to trust a woman."

"What do you know of women, old man?" Griff snorted.

"Enough to live alone," the old man retorted, and then cackled. Griff couldn't help grinning, even when Bridget elbowed him in the side.

"Everything around us, everything we can touch, taste, feel—it's all a woman." Raghnall dropped him a wink. "And it's all magic."

"It's flowin' around us all the time." Bridget turned in his arms. "Like the wind. Like love."

"But I do'na trust it..." Griff frowned.

"Ye trust me," she whispered, reaching up to cup his face in her hands, bringing him in to kiss her.

He nodded as they parted, confessing hoarsely, "Aye."

"You're learning, wulver..." Raghnall chuckled.

Bridget went to the chair, pulling out a new pair of soft, silver and white boots and putting them on. Clearly a gift from the mage. Then he watched her slip a silver dirk into them under her new robes.

"Do they all look like angels an' fight like devils?" Griff wondered aloud.

"No." Raghnall grinned. "Some look like devils and fight like angels."

Griff laughed at that.

"Now let's eat so we can start our journey," Raghnall said, getting up from the table.

"I do'na mind ye taggin' along," Griff said as they followed the old man out. "But... why're ye comin' wit' us?"

"Would you like me to talk more about destiny?" Raghnall asked, glancing over his shoulder.

"No." Griff snorted.

"Let's just say... I'll be stopping off on Skara Brae before I take a journey with some old friends."

Could the old man be any more cryptic? Griff wondered.

He caught Bridget around the waist before they followed Raghnall in toward the delicious smell of food. "You'll hafta change outta that before we reach t'ship... more's the pity."

"D'ye like it?" Bridget smiled, putting her arms around his neck. "I do'na think t'will be necessary."

Griff frowned. "But t'pirates think yer a lad—and I'd like to keep 'em thinkin' that, t'tell t'truth!"

"Trust the magic, son." Raghnall just grinned that toothless old grin when Griff scowled in his direction.

But he didn't think about it overlong, because the food smelled amazing—and he was starving.

The Sea Wolf was there waiting for them to return, but it was surrounded by more than a dozen massive warships.

They were huge, Viking by the looks of them, with wolf heads on the prow.

"Slow up." Griff reined in the horse when they were a half-mile away, assessing the situation.

"Trust the magic," Raghnall said from the saddle of his mule. He was leading another behind him, loaded with a very full trunk. The old man chortled and winked, taking far too much pleasure in being cryptic, as far as Griff was concerned.

"I wish ye'd both stop sayin' that." Griff grimaced. "Ye want me t'just ride into a trap?"

"Tis not a trap." Bridget, still wearing her silver robe and riding sidesaddle in front of him, spoke up. "Those are wulver ships."

"There's no such thing as a—" Griff frowned as the wind shifted, and he lifted his nose in the air. Wulvers. She was right. He could smell them, even this far off.

"Wulvers are warriors, not sailors," Griff protested, but thoughts of the lost packs spurred him on.

He couldn't get to the shoreline fast enough—and the old man and his mules slowed them way down. By the time they reached the shoreline, Captain Blackburn was on the deck with a spyglass, awaiting their arrival. Clearly, he'd been in contact with the other ships. Whatever it meant, Griff didn't like it. He really didn't like it when a dozen men appeared from behind the rocks as they approached. Griff already had his sword drawn, but he knew, even though they weren't shifted, that they were all wulvers.

"No! Wait!" Griff called, but Raghnall had broken away, his mule moving faster than it had the whole trip as he rode forward to speak to the men. "Stupid ol' man."

Then the wulvers drew their swords. He had visions of the old man being slaughtered by a dozen wulvers as he leapt off his horse, leaving Bridget safely behind as he advanced, sword raised, ready to take them all on at once. He felt the heat in his own eyes, saw it reflected in the eyes of the men who looked at him as he approached.

"Easy, warrior." Raghnall gave him a toothless grin.

And then, one by one, each wulver sank to one knee, driving their swords into the sand, hands on the hilts as they bowed their heads before him.

Griff stared, looking first at the grinning Raghnall, then back at the kneeling wulvers.

"Do'na leave me again!" Bridget snapped as she rode up behind him, reining in the horse. Then she stopped, staring at the kneeling wulver men.

"What?" Raghnall chuckled. "You two have never seen wulvers offer their swords and fealty before?"

Griff looked at Bridget, feeling a lump growing in his throat, and then back at the men who knelt before him.

"You can't leave them down there all night, son," Raghnall whispered, nudging him.

Griff cleared his throat. "Rise."

He blinked as they all got to their feet. The biggest one, a wulver warrior with long, thick blonde hair—Griff knew he'd be a giant, white wolf when he shifted—stepped forward, holding out a gloved hand.

"Lars." The blonde said his name in a heavy, Scandanavian accent.

"Griff." He took the other wulver's hand and shook it, feeling the power in the man's grip.

"We are ready to sail and fight for you," Lars told him. "You are the red wulver. You are our king."

"Thank ye." Griff cleared his throat—it wasn't easy talking around the lump in it. "I'm proud t'have yer service. I'm grateful for all of ye who've come t'serve me."

He spoke this last to all of the wulvers gathered on the beach.

Bridget had slipped off the horse and came to stand beside Griff. He glanced down, seeing the part down the center of her red head as she looked out at all the wulvers who had come to serve him.

Then, one by one, they lined up to bow in front of Bridget, all of them reaching out to touch her hand or kiss it, murmuring the words, "My queen."

When Bridget looked up at him, her green eyes were round and sparkling with tears. She accepted each one of them with the grace of a queen. She was, already, as far as he was concerned. She had been, since the first time he'd met her. Even wearing armor.

"Griff," she whispered, turning her face up to him. "Is this one of t'lost packs?"

He nodded, sure of it, even though they hadn't said. One of the places Aleesa had given him was across the sea, and he was sure these wulvers were Vikings of some sort. He'd never seen them before, but they were all ready to lay down their lives for him.

And, he had a feeling, as they got ready to sail back to Skara Brae, he was going to need them.

"Trust the magic yet?" Bridget whispered, putting her arms around him.

"Aye, lass." He smiled into her hair, watching the men—*his men*—returning to their ships.

Did he have a choice anymore? He wondered. Had he ever?

They got into one of the wulver rowboats and headed toward the Sea Wolf where Captain Blackburn was waiting for them. The two wulver oarsmen helped them out of the boat and onto the ship.

"Next time yer sendin' a wulver welcome party, lemme know, eh?" Captain Blackburn called as Griff approached. The big sea captain was grinning from ear to ear.

"I did'na know," Griff confessed, shaking the captain's outstretched hand.

"If they'd been enemies, t'Sea Wolf woulda been at t'bottom of t'bay by now." Blackburn snorted, looking behind them at the big, wulver oarsmen as they boarded, but his gaze kept returning to Bridget.

"Aren't ye gonna ask who t'woman is?" Griff put an arm around Bridget, pulling her close.

"Ye think we've ne'er seen a woman disguised as a man for passage on a ship before?" The captain snorted. "She ne'er passed, e'en when ye carried her on wrapped in her plaid. That hair alone…"

"Aye." Griff looked down at her, smiling. "I could'na bear t'cut it."

"Would've been a terrible sacrifice," the captain agreed with a shake of his salt and pepper head. "Right *Bryce*—and *Busby*."

Griff laughed. "It's Griff."

The captain gave a knowing nod, looking at Bridget, while Griff made the introductions.

"Busby played by the beautiful Bridget. This old gentleman is Raghnall. And this…" Griff turned to the two Scandanavian wulvers with a questioning look.

"Thorvel," said one, and, "Skald," said the other.

"Yer takin' this rather well," Griff remarked to the captain.

"Well, we did 'ave a message of warnin' an' promise of payment." Blackburn laughed. Just then, Raghnall's owl flew down from the mast above, landing lightly on the old man's shoulder. "MacMoran almos' shot 'im fer dinner before we realized he was carryin' a message."

Griff caught the old man's eye—Raghnall's toothless grin gave him away.

"Will ye be boardin' yer ship, then?" Griff asked Thorvel and Skald, but the two wulvers insisted on staying with Griff, which meant more to him than he could possibly say.

The room he stayed in with Bridget as they sailed toward Skara Brae was far better than the one they'd occupied on the way to the Isle of the Dragon. Not that Griff and Bridget saw much of the room. Of course, they didn't see much more than the room, either.

Thorvel and Skald took turns standing guard outside, but the door only opened a few times to admit trays of food and drink to keep up their energy.

Which was just the way Griff intended it.

Because once he got Bridget out of that stunning silver and white robe, he knew he wasn't going to let her put it back on again—until he had to.

Chapter Ten

"I'm not stayin', Griff, and that's final!" Bridget stomped her foot on the rocky shoreline. Not that stamping her foot in soft slippers under her silvery robes had the same effect as doing so when she wore armor and boots. "Besides, Raghnall told me—"

"Bridget, this is war, not magic!" Griff roared. "You're stayin' here where ye'll be safe, and that's final!"

"Tis mos' certainly not final!" she snapped. "Tis m'kin, too, ye big oaf!"

"Bridget, I swear by all that is holy, if ye defy me..."

"Griff." Darrow rode up on his big war horse, reining it in when he saw Bridget. "T'men are ready, as y'ordered."

"Thank ye," Griff replied, surveying the encampment. Bridget could almost see his mind working.

They'd landed on the east side of the isle, hoping that Uldred was still camped on the west side, and their gamble had been correct. Bridget frowned up at Darrow. They'd been introduced, and she knew the man was Raife's brother. He'd been one of the few who hadn't been captured inside the temple.

The thought of that sick, twisted monster and his witch of a mother holding her family hostage made Bridget crazy with rage. She wanted to storm in there, sword drawn, but she knew that wasn't what needed to happen. Raghnall had been very clear on that point. They'd talked long, while Griff slept off the poison cure. The poor man had been through so much worrying about Bridget's wounds, he hadn't even realized how effected he'd been by the stuff. Until he passed out and slept for a good thirty hours!

"Griff, I wan' ye t'think this through," Darrow cautioned, leaning over the neck of his horse to talk to his nephew. "Remember what yer father taught ye—about doin' somethin' yerself that could get ye killed."

"Aye, I know." Griff waved this away, like he'd waved Bridget's protests away. "Like m'father send someone else into the temple, instead of goin' in 'imself?"

Darrow sighed, straightening in his saddle. "Alaric rode out t'meet 'im, I told ye. How were we t'know Uldred's men had entered the temple while Aleesa was alone."

Bridget cringed at this. The thought of Uldred's men storming into the temple while Aleesa was left, defenseless, made her stomach turn. When Raife and his men—and, it turned out, women, because Sibyl, Laina and Kirstin had insisted on coming with them—had been out meeting with Alaric, one of Uldred's men had feigned need of healing at the temple. Without Alaric there as guardian, Aleesa had unknowingly let him in. That was all the opening they needed. When Alaric returned with Raife and the rest of the wulver party, the temple had already been infiltrated.

Bridget couldn't believe the women had come too, but apparently, after Rory MacFalon had been captured—the same day Griff had left to go to Skara Brae, it turned out—Raife and Donal MacFalon had made plans to go find their sons. They'd assumed they'd run off together, some young pup's idea of sowing their wild oats perhaps, but the truth had been much darker than that.

Darrow said they'd pried it out of Moira and Beitrus, how they'd fed Griff information about the lost packs on Skara Brae, and they assumed he'd taken Rory with him. It was only after Raife and everyone had gone into the temple—and the scouts rode back to tell Darrow, who had stayed back on the beach with several of the men on Raife's orders, of the encampment on the other side of the island— that they knew Rory had been captured by Uldred's men.

Bridget still felt horribly guilty about leaving him behind. They'd intended to rescue him, but the witch's poison blade had put an end to that. Thankfully, Darrow and the few wulvers who had been left behind had raided Uldred's camp and rescued Rory MacFalon. He was, right then, recovering from his many wounds in a tent not too far from where they were talking.

"Do'na sacrifice yerself," Darrow said, trying one last time to convince his nephew not to follow through with this plan.

"I hafta." Griff shook his dark head. "It has t'be me. The prophecy..."

"T'hell wit' the prophecy!" Darrow roared, rolling his eyes. "This isn't magic, this is war!"

Bridget smirked, seeing the look of surprise on Griff's face. Hadn't he just yelled that at her, when she told him she had to accompany him to the temple?

"Bridget." Griff turned to her with a soft sigh. "Ye'll ride wit' me."

"Yer takin' a woman!" Darrow groaned.

But Bridget's heart soared. She knew, then, that he believed. At least to some degree. Enough to acknowledge that he needed her, not just because she knew where all the secret entrances to the temple were, but because she was part of this. They needed to go to the sacred pool together, during the eclipse, or everything would fall apart. Everything they'd done, everything they'd worked for, everything that had, so far, fallen in place, if not perfectly, then with some semblance of order and balance—all of that would disintegrate into nothing.

"I hafta." Griff sighed again, turning toward the tent. "Rory! Garaith! I need ye!"

And so their small little band was set. Rory, Garaith, Griff and Bridget would ride, alone, to the temple.

They would sneak in the back, secret entrance.

Griff, of course, thought they were going to simply surprise Uldred and his men, slay them, and free the wulver prisoners they'd taken.

Bridget knew better. The eclipse was coming, and with it, Griff's destiny. She caught Raghnall's eye across the beach, saw him watching, as always. He didn't always speak—and when he did, he often sounded mad, or addled—but he knew the truth, as well as she did. Things had fallen just the way they were supposed to. Everything, including her own near-death, had done nothing but propel them to this moment in time.

The thought made her tremble with both excitement and fear.

All is as it should be.

Mayhaps, if she kept repeating that to herself, it truly would be.

She hoped so.

Because she'd never been more terrified in her life.

She'd only known about the secret temple entrance for a few years. As a child, she thought it was magical when Alaric would appear during one of their rituals at the scrying pool. And it was, to some degree. The entrance was enchanted, made to appear as solid rock from one side, but a cavernous opening from the other. Alaric had shown it to her after the first time she'd bested him during training. It had been a wonderful reward, and Bridget enjoyed surprising Aleesa by showing up for rituals that way afterward. Until Aleesa got used to her using it, of course, and it became old hat.

Still, it always tended to be a shock, when someone appeared to walk through a solid rock wall.

"Yer sure they can'na hear us," Rory whispered. His words were slurred. His mouth was still healing. Uldred's men had made quite a sport of torturing the lad. Daily. Sometimes several times a day, since he had such enormous healing capacity. It was the cruelest thing she could imagine. If there'd been some score to settle that Uldred had been playing out with The MacFalon's only son, they were now more than even.

"Aye," Bridget replied, but she kept her voice down anyway. She'd tested it hundreds of times, yelling her mother's name—she could see Aleesa during these little sessions but Aleesa, of course, couldn't see her—and there'd never been any indication that she could see or hear anything until Bridget stepped across the threshold.

"Garaith, Rory." Griff unsheathed his sword. "Use the manacles I gave ye and chain Bridget over there."

"What?" Bridget gasped as Rory, looking quite guilty about it, and Garaith, who was nearly as tall and handsome as Griff, but not quite, took her, one at each elbow.

"I'm sorry." Griff sighed. "I needed ye to get us in 'ere, but Bridget... I can'na risk ye. Trust me."

"No!" she wailed, as Rory locked a manacle on one of her wrists, Garaith the other. It happened too fast, and she was too stunned to draw her sword and parry. "Griff, listen t'me! Ye do'na understand! Ye need me!"

"Aye." He sighed, surveying the gathering at the scrying pool. It was nearing noon. Nearing the eclipse.

Uldred and his witch-mother, Moraga, were talking by the edge of the pool. Across from them, all of the wulvers were chained, like an audience, to the stone monoliths. Seeing her mother and father chained was like a sharp stab to the heart. She didn't recognize any of the others, but she knew they were Griff's kin who had come to look for him.

"Griff!" Bridget cried, and he turned, coming over to her, shouldering Rory and Garaith out of the way. He pulled her to him one-armed—he held his sword in the other—and kissed her.

She knew he was kissing her goodbye. She knew, if he walked through that opening and left her behind, it would be a true goodbye. She'd never see him again. Things would fall apart, would succumb to the dark forces that had been working against them all along. And she couldn't let that happen.

"I need t'keep ye safe," Griff whispered against her ear as they parted. She was breathless with his desperate, aching kiss, heart racing in her chest. "Please, m'love, stay 'ere. I can'na bear t'lose ye."

"Look at me." She lifted her manacled hands, the chain that one of the other wulvers had locked to a ring in the wall, clinking loudly as she cupped his face in her palms. "Griff... I love ye."

She saw his face fall at her words, saw how they pierced his heart.

"An' I know ye love me."

"Aye," he agreed hoarsely. "I do love ye, lass. More than m'own life."

"Then trust me," she whispered, feeling tears stinging her eyes. She sensed Rory and Garaith watching this exchange. They hung back, waiting. "Trust t'magic. Can ye do that? Fer me? Please?"

"Bridget..." He croaked her name, shaking his head, the pain in his eyes breaking her heart. "Do'na ask this o'me..."

"I hafta." She kissed his lips, tasting the salt of her tears. "Ye mus' take me wit' ye. Ye mus'! If ye do'na, this ends 'ere. It all—e'erything—ends. Right 'ere."

Griff closed his eyes for a moment, sighing again. Then he took a long, slow, shuddering breath, and turned to go.

"Griff!" Bridget wailed, watching him walk toward the pool, toward the secret entrance. "Please! Trust me!"

He stopped, and she saw past him, into the cavern beyond. She saw Moraga pointing, whispering something to her son, whose eyes narrowed as he glanced toward the wall. It seemed as if he was looking straight at her and Bridget shrank back.

Griff looked over his shoulder, meeting her eyes. There was so much pain in them. And they were blood red.

"Unchain her," he whispered hoarsely, glancing at his friends.

"But... ye said—" Garaith frowned, looking at Rory.

"Unchain her!" Griff snapped.

Bridget fell to her knees, tears streaming down her face, holding her hands up to Rory as he came over with the key.

"Oh good, one of them's already chained up." Uldred's voice filled the cavern, but it was coming from the other side of the pool.

Bridget looked up, seeing the witch, her mouth moving, incanting, and she understood what had happened. She didn't know how, but the witch had discovered them, and had revealed their hiding place. She heard a woman scream, and saw a redhead across the way, one of the women chained to the rock. Griff's mother, she guessed. He'd told her they were both redheads. She called her son's name as his sword swung, clashing with Uldred's.

Rory and Garaith came out swinging, too, and Bridget reached for her own sword, realizing she didn't have one—Rory and Garaith had taken it—but she had her dirk. She slipped it out of her boot, ready to defend her family, when she heard Uldred yell at them all to, "Stop!"

Griff didn't. His sword came down again, steel clashing. There had never been weapons at the sacred pool before. Bridget saw her mother sobbing, Alaric doing his best to comfort her, both of them in chains.

"Stop, dog, or I'll kill them all!" Uldred snapped.

That stopped Griff. He faced the dark knight, both of them breathing hard, and saw that Uldred's men had blades at the throats of the women chained across the way. Bridget saw they were all collared and muzzled—they'd been prepared, then, for the wulvers to shift, and had guarded against it.

"Chain them with the rest," Uldred ordered, giving Griff a sly smile as the men disengaged their swords.

"Trust," Bridget whispered to Griff as she passed by, glaring at Uldred.

Griff's eyes were already glowing red, Bridget saw, as one of Uldred's men dragged her around the pool to join the others. He howled as he saw her being chained to one of the high monoliths and Uldred laughed. The witch stood well out of the way of the wulvers, Bridget noted, but she was smiling, triumphant. She believed she and her son had already won.

Lifting her head to look up at the domed ceiling, Bridget wondered if mayhaps they had.

Trust.

That's what she'd told Griff, but that's what she had to do, as well.

Everything in her wanted to fight. But she had to watch, wait, and trust.

Above them the light was already changing. It was nearly full noon, but instead of a bright beam of light shining into the scrying pool, it was fading. The eclipse had already begun.

"Let them go!" Griff demanded. Uldred hadn't forced the big wulver to give up his sword and Bridget wondered at that.

"You're not in much of a position to make demands." Uldred smiled across the pool, and he looked right at Bridget. She felt his gaze on her, almost as if his eyes raking her body was actually the touch of his hands, and it made her shudder with disgust. "I think I'm going to enjoy your little redheaded whore later myself. I'll let my men have the other women. I prefer my cunts wetter than those old prunes."

Griff growled, giving a shake of his head, and shifted. Bridget gasped, watching him leap forward as a wulver-warrior, sword swinging, but Uldred turned just in time to stop the blow with his own sword.

"You want a fight, is that it?" Uldred pushed hard at the big wulver, although he didn't move Griff far. More of Uldred's men—there were at least a dozen in the temple, all human, Bridget counted—moved in, swords drawn. "A duel? If you win, you get your woman and family as a reward? Is that what you want, dog?"

Griff just snarled, his eyes so red they glowed, even in the fading light. He had four men behind him, holding him back, and Bridget cried out when she felt one of Uldred's men move in beside her, holding a knife to her throat. Griff heard, his gaze skipping across the pool to her.

"But what if I win?" Uldred actually smiled. "If I win...
let's say, I get to use your blood. And all those wulvers out
there..."

The dark knight waved his hand toward the wall,
beyond which were hundreds of wulvers from the lost
packs.

"Then they will follow me. Oh wait, once I look into the
pool during the eclipse, I'll turn into the red wulver, and
they'll follow me anyway, won't they?" Uldred gave a
gleeful, mad laugh, and Bridget saw that the man was, in
part, mad. He had to be. Given what Griff had told her about
Uldred and Moraga's plans—had the witch made her own
son mad with power? Like his father before him, he was
obsessed with the wulvers, but he didn't want to kill them.
No—*Uldred wanted to become one of them.* And his mother
had convinced him it was possible. Had convinced him that
they shared a bloodline.

Of course, that part was true. Raghnall had told her as
much, while Griff was still sleeping off the poison, but she
hadn't wanted to reveal that to him. She knew he wouldn't
take it very well—and it didn't seem to serve much of a
purpose. The fact was, Uldred was not and would never be a
wulver, no matter whose blood ran through his veins. While
Eldred, his father before him, had been sure he was part of
Arthur's line, that the Tudors had stolen the throne and
wrongly changed the bloodline of England's kings forever,
Uldred seemed far more interested in gaining the wulvers'
abilities and powers and using them to his advantage.

Eldred had wanted to use the wulvers and destroy them.

Uldred wanted to become a wulver—and enslave them.

"Let's fight, brother, as men!" Uldred laughed,
swinging his sword around, and Griff managed to lift his to
block the blow, even though four of Uldred's men held him
back, and Uldred knocked his sword from his hands. Griff
growled and went for it, but the men held him back. "And
when I spill your blood into this pool, I will become the

most powerful wulver—the most powerful king and leader—this world has ever known!"

Griff shifted back as Uldred reached down to grab Griff's sword, tossing it back to him, and when he did, Bridget saw it happen. She wasn't sure, not at first, but she saw a flash of silver in the dimming light coming in from the dome above. A blade? Griff gave a little howl and Uldred stepped back with a shrug, as if to ask, 'What did I do?'

But then the men were fighting, and there was no time to think.

Or even breathe.

Bridget covered her mouth with her hands, feeling an arm go around her. It was her mother, standing beside her, comforting her. Bridget let her arms slide around her mother's neck as she watched the two men fighting. Griff's eyes flashed red as their swords swung, chipping away at the stone walls when they missed, clashing angrily when they didn't.

Griff's eyes glowed a deep red but he stayed in human form, not shifting to his stronger, wulver one. Bridget saw Uldred's smile, the way he danced back and forth, avoiding Griff's heavy blows. And she saw his eyes glow red, too. A trick of the light, mayhaps? She was sure of it. A reflection of Griff's eyes in his own.

Griff was growing tired. She expected him to shift to wulver form, to take the man out in one mighty blow, but he didn't. He stumbled once, nearly falling into Uldred, and the other man pushed him back. Bridget clung to her mother, watching Griff losing the fight, sinking to her knees in horror as Griff reeled and swung, almost blindly.

They swung their way around the pool, drawing closer to the chained pack of wulvers—and humans—adorning the rock, Bridget among them. She sobbed into her mother's robes as Griff howled, the sound echoing through the whole chamber, shaking it to its foundation, while Uldred just laughed and danced away.

Bridget knew it was close. It was almost time. Moraga knew it too. The witch was on the other side of the pool, staring up at the hole in the ceiling and chanting something. Griff was fighting Uldred off now—bleeding from several wounds, deep gashes that would take a little time to heal. Uldred backed him up, swinging again and again, then took a step forward, swords sliding together, down to their hilts as they stood, face to face. Bridget was so close to them, she could have reached out and touched the wound bleeding on Griff's calf.

Then Uldred pushed Griff away, and the big man fell.

He fell to his knees, right in front of Bridget, and she reached out for him, unable to bear seeing him in so much pain. It made no sense, no sense at all. He was ten times the man, twenty times the warrior, of this man, and yet, Griff was flagging, failing.

"Trust…" Griff lifted his head to look into her eyes and Bridget saw how dilated his were.

"Ye monster!" she gasped, staring at Uldred. "Ye poisoned 'im!"

Just the flash of a blade, a small cut on his calf. Uldred had poisoned him, making sure he'd win this fight. Griff struggled to stand, but whatever it was Uldred had knicked him with was strong.

"Just a little help from *Natura Mater*, eh, Mother?" Uldred laughed, glancing across the pool at the witch.

"He's right." Bridget looked at Griff. "Mother Nature decides. That's 'er magic. We need t'trust 'er."

"Uldred!" Moraga snapped. "Stop playin' around! Tis time!"

Uldred practically skipped past them as the eclipse began to reach its peak. It wouldn't be long. Griff growled, turning to rise, to go after Uldred, but Bridget slipped her hand into his.

Trust.

"Trust," she whispered to him, squeezing. Holding him back, holding him to her.

"No!" Griff croaked, still on his knees.

Uldred was on his too, but he was on hands and knees, peering over the edge into the pool, as if waiting for something. Uldred's men murmured, uneasy. The light in the pool was strange, unlike anything Bridget had ever seen before.

"Noooo!" Griff cried again as the dragon's head began to rise.

Bridget cried out, grabbing his shoulders as Griff started forward. His body shook, wracked with the poison. Aleesa went to her knees, too, grabbing his arm, keeping him from confronting Uldred.

Uldred's men began to pray under their breath, some of them crossing themselves as the dragon's head filled the space above the pool. And turned its red eyes to Uldred.

"Look at his eyes!" one of Uldred's men cried. "Look!"

Uldred's eyes were blood red as he stared, transfixed, at the dragon. Across the pool, Moraga laughed, a high, delighted cackle. Bridget heard sobs, and glanced at the wulvers and women still chained to the rock. A dark-haired woman sobbed into the shoulder of a man. The redheaded woman Bridget assumed was Griff's mother, Sibyl, was looking, not at Uldred and the dragon, but at Griff and Bridget on their knees by the pool. She had tears in her eyes.

"It's happening!" Uldred called. "Oh, Mother, it's happening! I can feel it! I'm turning into the red wulver!"

Griff howled, the sound reverberating against the stone walls, and Bridget shivered at the sound, holding his hand so tight it hurt her own. She couldn't keep her eyes off Uldred, the way his eyes glowed red. Was it really true, then? The prophecy… could it be that either of these men could be the red wulver, able to bring together the lost packs, and heal the rift between man and wulver forever?

But it couldn't be—Raghnall had been so sure. Uldred couldn't be the one. His magic was dark, his purpose less than honorable. But if he was a descendent of Arthur—or

Asher—then mayhaps it was possible for him to usurp that role. To become the once and future king of… everything.

"Look!" Sibyl gasped, pointing at Uldred. "He's on fire!"

Bridget stared as the red of the man's eyes spread. They were on fire, glowing, hot, and Uldred laughed, holding his arms out to the dragon as if in welcome. Didn't he feel it? It wasn't just his eyes—his whole body was outlined in flame!

Moraga screamed. "Uldred! Uldred! Noooo!"

"Mother!" The man screamed as he went to his knees, his body beginning to burn.

They all stared in horror as the witch threw herself at her son, sobbing, calling his name over and over—but that didn't last long.

Once the fire had begun, it burned hot and fast, consuming everything around it. Even one of Uldred's men, who tried to pull the two apart, was burned up in the flame. It was over in moments. The screaming stopped, and then the fire did, too. There was simply nothing left of either Uldred or Moraga.

But the dragon was still there, head raised.

And then, slowly, it turned to look at them.

"Unchain them," Bridget croaked to Uldred's man standing closest to her. She pulled her dirk from her boot and pointed it at him. "Do it now, and ye might live through this."

The man, white as a sheet and still staring as the dragon turned its red eyes in their direction, did as she bid him.

"Quickly." Aleesa bent to assist her daughter, once she was free. Bridget helped Griff toward the pool. He moved slowly, groggy. Whatever poison Uldred had used was very bad for wulvers, and Bridget worried that even the sacred pool wouldn't be able to heal him.

"Bridget," he murmured, on his knees, wavering.

"I'm 'ere." She slipped her hand into his, feeling tears sliding down her cheeks, realizing that this might be the last time they were ever together.

"I love ye," he whispered, and she felt him lean against her for support. He was fading fast. "Yer... m'one... true... mate..."

Bridget sobbed, clinging to him, feeling hands on her, holding her up, too, otherwise she would have collapsed as well. They were all around them, wulvers and humans, hands on their shoulders, under their elbows, holding them both, supporting them, and Bridget looked up, gasping at what faced her in the pool.

It wasn't just the dragon.

There was the most beautiful woman she'd ever seen, full figured and smiling, her eyes shining silver, staring straight at Bridget. She heard a collective gasp, heard one of Uldred's men moan, "Her eyes! Her eyes, too!" but she knew. She felt her own eyes flash silver in response, a cool, calm feeling of peace coming over her as the lady approached.

The woman carried a sword, blade high as she walked across the pool.

Beside her, the dragon, eyes glowing red, like blood though, not fire, opened its mouth.

For a moment, Bridget thought they were all going to burn.

But then the dragon's tongue uncoiled, and at the end of it was a chalice. It dipped first into the sacred pool, and then it was placed in Griff's hands. The big wulver was shaking so badly he could barely grasp it, but his mother and aunts were there, helping him drink.

Bridget looked up just in time to accept the sword. The lady held it aloft, hilt resting on one palm, blade the other. An offering. Bridget looked up into her face, into those strange, silver eyes, and saw her own. For one, brief moment, as she reached out to accept the sword, they merged.

Bridget gave a cry, her whole body shaking, the sword clattering to the stone where she knelt, and then, they were gone. The dragon and the lady disappeared. The peak of the eclipse had passed. The marriage of Asher and Ardis was over.

She lifted her eyes to the sun, to the strange light overhead. It was the middle of the day, but it felt as if the moon were shining down, and it filled her with an overwhelming urge. Bridget threw back her head and howled.

It was only then that she realized, she was a wolf. She had no hands to hold a sword. Only big, russet colored paws. Stunned, she turned to look at Griff, and saw, he, too, had shifted. Not into a wulver warrior, but into full wolf form. Their eyes met—flashing red and silver for just a moment—before they rubbed noses together, and then Bridget tucked her head under his, a sign of surrender.

She was his, and always would be.

They were one, true mates, just as Ardis and Asher had been. In this form, she knew it in a way she'd never known it before. If she had been a wolf the moment they met, she wouldn't have ever questioned it. She was his. She belonged to this man.

Griff shook his head, giving a long, sustained howl, and she watched him change. Thick, red fur became long, dark hair. His eyes went from red to gold again. He stood there, naked, surrounded by his kin, holding a hand out to her. He saw her, he recognized her. He loved her. They gave him his plaid, and he wrapped it around himself, looking at her expectantly, smiling.

Bridget did what came naturally. She gave her big, russet colored wolf's head a shake, and transformed. Her mother was there, putting a robe around her shoulders, and she threw her shaking arms around Griff's neck, unable to fully comprehend what was happening. Had she really just changed into a wolf—and back again? What did it mean?

"M'love," Griff whispered against her ear, holding her close. He was so solid, so strong. Nothing about him wavered now. The sacred pool had healed him. And it had, somehow, changed her. "M'one true mate."

"Aye," she breathed, clinging to him. "Took ye long enough to b'lieve it, wulver."

He chuckled. "Look who's talkin'—*wulver.*"

That's when she heard it.

Whispered, murmured words, all around them.

She looked at Griff, disbelieving at first, and then, Griff took her hand, turning toward his subjects, turning her with him, to face them all. Even Uldred's own men. Mayhaps, sometimes seeing was believing, Bridget thought with her own sense of amazement.

"Righ."

"Banrighinn."

King.

Queen.

Bridget stared as, one by one, wulver and human took a knee and bowed their heads to the once and future king and queen.

The End

Bridget had always thought of Skara Brae as home, but it wouldn't be for much longer.

Still, this room, the place where she'd first made love with her one true mate, would always hold great meaning for her. She crouched by the fireplace, warming her hands around the cup of milk she held. It had done a great deal lately to settle her stomach at night, especially nights like these, when she dreamed of the lady and couldn't sleep.

"Bridget." Griff called out, his hand searching her side of the bed for her and she smiled.

"I'm 'ere," she called softly.

"Come t'bed, lass."

She finished the last of her milk, leaving the cup on the table, before climbing in beside him.

"Up dreamin' of weddin' plans?" He chuckled, sliding his arm around her waist and pulling her near. She gave a happy sigh, snugging back against his warmth.

"Oh, I do'na need t'plan a thin'." She smiled. "Yer mother and m'mother are takin' care of't. All I need t'do is put on t'dress."

"And then I get t'take it off ye." His hand moved slowly over her hip, under the covers.

"Mmm, aye," she agreed, feeling him growing hard against her bottom. "Will it be a long trip back to Scotland?"

"Not overlong." His hand stroked her hip, a soothing motion. "Are y'afeared t'leave this place?"

"A lil," she admitted softly.

"If it's any consolation, t'mountain den'll be new t'me, too, lass." His lips brushed her temple. "But we've got s'many wulvers now that the lost packs have joined us, we need the room. And the witch who kept us from it is…"

"Aye." Her eyes narrowed as she looked into the fire. "Gone."

Besides, even if the witch hadn't burned up with Uldred in the fire, they now knew how to enchant the entrance to any den, the same way they did the temples, and they would simply disappear. No human would ever know they were there. Only wulver eyes would be able to see them, and only when they wanted to be seen.

They were quiet for a moment and then Bridget laughed. "Wolf packs. Raghnall loves his word play."

"Aye, t'old codger." Griff grunted, not sounding anywhere near as amused as she was.

Griff had talked overlong about the lost wolf packs, had set out to find them, had asked the old mage about them, when all along, it was wolf *pax*. It wasn't even wolf pact, if you traced the line far back enough. Raghnall had gleefully told them that there had been many translations of the prophecy over the years since the Latin translation that brought together the rest during the Roman reign of Constantine.

Raghnall had relayed that even the "wolf pact" they lived under was once known as the Wolf Pax, which translated to the Wolf Peace. Translation and time turned it from a time of peace to a treaty to prevent war. A subtle difference, mayhaps, but a big one.

The lost packs Griff had been looking for was really "the wolf pax." The peace the wulvers would live under, once the prophecy was fulfilled.

"D'ye wanna be more involved in plannin' t'wedding, then?" Griff asked. "Is that what keeps y'up a'nigh'?"

"Nay." Bridget snorted. "I'm more interested in trainin' than wearin' a dress. Besides, it brings all t'women together and gives 'em somethin' else t'do besides cook."

"Aleesa and Kirstin seem t'be gettin' along well," Griff said softly, treading carefully.

She knew it might seem like a sore spot, her adopted mother reuniting with her blood-born daughter, but Bridget didn't begrudge them any of the time they spent, the things they now shared together. She was happy for them both.

And that Kirstin's son, Rory, was back to his old wulver self, all healed—at least, physically. And Aleesa was getting to know her grandson, and her son-in-law, The MacFalon, as well as her daughter.

"Aye, I'm glad," she said, truthfully. "Aleesa's been so busy teachin' Sibyl how t'be temple priestess, she's spreadin' herself thin. But I think she loves havin' everyone around, after being alone s'long."

"I'm still reelin' over that." Griff sighed.

Bridget put a hand over his on her hip. "I know y'are… but doesn't it seem fittin', somehow, that Raife and Sibyl will stay here in the temple as the new guardian and priestess?"

"I s'pose." Griff sounded doubtful.

"They were both called t'do it," she reminded him. Griff had come a long way when it came to believing in things like magic and prophecies and one true mates—but the idea of being "called" into service in the temple was still a stretch for him. "And we can come visit. We will, all t'time."

"Aye," he agreed. "And I'm ready t'lead the pack. I think it's one of the real reasons they decided t'stay here. So there'd be no conflict…"

"They love ye," she reminded him. "And they know tis time."

"When does Raghnall get back?" he wondered aloud, changing the subject.

"Before t'weddin', I hope." She smiled to herself. "He'll be the closest thing to a grandfather t'bairn'll have. At least on m'side."

She smiled, remembering that day when Raghnall had sat her down, while Griff slept off the poison, and told her how he'd found her, abandoned, at the door of the temple on the Isle of the Dragon. It had been the one time Aleesa and Alaric had met Raghnall—when he brought her to them to raise. He said he knew she was part of the prophecy, somehow. That she was fated to be trained as the temple guardian and priestess on Skara Brae.

Bridget still didn't know who her parents were—but Aleesa and Alaric were wulver, like she was now. They loved her, had raised her—and she didn't mind anymore that she didn't know her parentage. Besides, when she'd asked Raghnall about them before he left on his journey to meet up with the Dragon and the Lady, he'd smiled and said, cryptically, "There is always more to the story, m'dear."

So mayhaps, someday, she would know.

"The... what?" Griff sat up on his elbow, staring down at her. "What did y'say?"

"Hm?" Bridget turned her head to look at him, feeling warm and sleepy from her milk.

"Did ye say... bairn?"

Bridget stopped breathing. "Did I?"

"Are ye wit' chil', lass?" Griff's eyes glowed red in the firelight. She loved when they did that.

"Aye," she breathed, biting her lip. "I was goin' t'wait after t'wedding to announce it but..."

"When were ye gonna tell me?" he growled, turning her toward him and putting a hand over her lower belly. It was slightly swollen, but she'd made the excuse that she was getting fat on all the cooking the wulver women did, and Griff hadn't questioned her.

"Now." She grinned, watching him pull the covers back and dip his head so he could kiss her navel.

"Asher," he murmured, flicking his tongue over her skin. "Or Ardis, if tis a girl."

"We could call him Arthur," she suggested with a smile. "If tis a *human* boy."

"But yer wulver now," he reminded her. "T'will surely be a wulver."

"I do'na know." She shrugged. "Everythin' has changed—but ye got me pregnant before I was wulver, y'ken?"

He chuckled. "Well, I s'pose it makes life interestin'. Donal and Kirstin are human parents who have a wulver child. We could be wulver parents who raise a human one."

"But Kirstin can change again," she reminded him. "All t'wulver women can change as they wish now."

That had been the part of the prophecy no one had understood, or translated, or seen coming. The cure for the wulver woman's curse had always lain with the dragon and the lady, with Asher and Ardis and their marriage. Somehow, Bridgit's transformation from human to wulver had completed a circle that had changed every wulver woman's curse of having to change, without warning, during her moon time, or during birth.

No wulver woman was a slave to her cycles anymore.

Darrow's wife, Laina, whose cycles had long since stopped, but whose daughters' were just beginning them, had wept like a child in his arms when they'd discovered this fact.

"Thank God fer that," Griff agreed, resting his cheek on her belly and looking up at her, his eyes a soft, glowing red in the firelight. "I'm really goin' t'be a father?"

"Aye." Her fingers tangled in his long, dark hair. "Are ye happy 'bout it?"

"Ye make me t'happiest wulver alive, lass." His hand moved up to cup her breast. "I ne'er would've b'lieved I could be s'happy in this or a thousand lifetimes."

"So are ye ready to tell me ye b'lieve in magic?" she teased. "In destiny? In prophecies? In one true mates...?"

"Do'na rub it in." He laughed, rolling his eyes. "Ye know I b'lieve... in *us*."

"Aye." She opened her arms and he went to her. It seemed that everything had worked the way it was supposed to after all. The prophecy was large, and they had played their parts, but according to the wulver—and human—women who read the text, it was still unfolding. Mayhaps it always would be, as Raghnall said, because everything was a circle that came around again.

But for now, all was as it should be.

At least, Bridget thought with a smile as Griff kissed his way over the swollen mound of her belly where little Ardis or Asher slept, dreamless...

Until the story continued...

THE BLOOD OF ANGELS

Sam has an unusual interest in humans, and considering she's a fairy of fate whose profession it is to determine their futures, it's no wonder! But it isn't just karma she's curious about. Sam has what her fairy-pal, Alex, thinks is an inordinate and rather wanton interest in certain biological aspects of human behavior—most notably, s-e-x!

When Sam's job leads her into the path of a handsome man who rocks her world, Sam's interest becomes obsession. Alex reminds her fairies get one Christmas wish. Will Sam consider using hers to become human just to experience one night of bliss?

But things aren't always what they seem. Zeph says he isn't like most… humans… and when Sam discovers who, and what, he really is, she's forced to make a choice that will transform her existence. Forever.

ABOUT SELENA KITT

Selena Kitt is a NEW YORK TIMES bestselling and award-winning author of erotic and romance fiction. She is one of the highest selling erotic writers in the business with over a million books sold!

Her writing embodies everything from the spicy to the scandalous, but watch out-this kitty also has sharp claws and her stories often include intriguing edges and twists that take readers to new, thought-provoking depths.

When she's not pawing away at her keyboard, Selena runs an innovative publishing company (excessica.com) and bookstore (excitica.com), as well as two erotica and erotic romance promotion companies (excitesteam.com and excitespice.com).

Her books EcoErotica (2009), The Real Mother Goose (2010) and Heidi and the Kaiser (2011) were all Epic Award Finalists. Her only gay male romance, Second Chance, won the Epic Award in Erotica in 2011. Her story, Connections, was one of the runners-up for the 2006 Rauxa Prize, given annually to an erotic short story of "exceptional literary quality."

She can be reached on her website at:

www.selenakitt.com

YOU'VE REACHED

"THE END!"